www.bookcabin.co.uk

Murder in a Parish Chest

Peggy Pinch Investigates

Malcolm Noble

Matador
9 Priory Business Park
Wistow Road
Kibworth Beauchamp
Leicester LE8 0RX, UK
Tel: (+44) 116 279 2299
Fax: (+44) 116 279 2277
Email: books@troubador.co.uk
Web: www.troubador.co.uk/matador

This is a work of fiction. All characters and events are imaginary
and any resemblance to actual characters and events is purely coincidental.

ISBN 978 1783060 566

British Library Cataloguing in Publication Data.
A catalogue record for this book is available from the British Library.

Typeset in 10.5pt Stempel Garamond by Troubador Publishing Ltd, Leicester, UK

Matador is an imprint of Troubador Publishing Ltd

Printed and bound in the UK by TJ International, Padstow, Cornwall

To Christine

PART ONE

CHAPTER ONE

The Night-time Adventures of a Village Policeman

Peggy's village was all talk. A mystery woman had been whispering with the old schoolma'am's lodger, the Becker wife was nowhere near when she should have been, and the policeman had fallen out with the Vicar.

Little Edie Snag, driven to be the conduit of all tidings, interrupted the pub cleaner with her worries and complaints, then hurried to the Vicarage garden where the maid was beating a rug on a line.

"He should listen to them as knows," Edie insisted, standing clear of the dust. "We always ring the church bell when something's wrong. Done it for a hundred years, we have." She had meant to say 'hundreds of years' but it was said now so she let it be.

The housemaid swiped with extra umph. "The Vicar knew that Tug Macaulay was on hand. He's the strongest man in our village. He showed quite enough muscle to bring that naughty Becker girl down from a tree."

"But Pinch said to ring it and he's our Constable."

"And the Vicar's the Vicar," said the housemaid. "Cedric Wells promised …"

Edie sang, "Well! Let's not listen to anything airy-fairy Wells says. He'll take any chance to trumpet his precious Macaulay."

"Now Edie, we don't want talk like that in the Vicar's garden, do we?"

Edie knew that she had lost her argument. She slapped her sides and sat down on the scullery step. "I just wish that PC Pinch had put the new Vicar in his place."

"Oh, Edie. Don't bother yourself. The Vicar's said something and you've taken it queer. Really, he doesn't want to spoil things."

"He said about my library."

"He doesn't want to close your library. It's the parish library."

Edie breathed deeply to stall her weeping. "Everyone says how good I've done it."

"And he'll say it too. You'll see."

"Bugger the Vicar." Constable Pinch took his pipe from his mouth so that he could mutter with more vigour. "Bugger his Verger, too." He stuck the blade of his spade into the summer soil and twisted it.

The Constable in his garden should have been a sentimental vignette of a country husband, somewhat out of condition, tending his little patch of England. A picture you might see on seasonal chapter headings about country life. A wagtail was perched on a fork handle not seven yards from Pinch's toil and Queen O' Scots, the schoolma'am's cat, was watching from the shed roof. Peggy, the policeman's young wife, came and went at the kitchen window as she completed her Thursday chores. But, that afternoon, Pinch was out of sorts. The outside edge of one foot was sore. The pain had nothing to do with his wellingtons or his fisherman's socks, and couldn't be blamed on his police boots; he had worn them for two years and they had never rubbed. No, Pinch was sure that his discomfort was due to bad humours of the body. Blood and water and … no need to go further. Pinch decided that his waters had been disrupted and that's what made the foot complain.

He had been in a sombre mood all day. He hadn't spoken at his regular breakfast in the gamekeeper's hut and, throughout the morning, he had patrolled the village quietly, hardly acknowledging familiar faces and avoiding those places where folk expected to see him. The War Memorial. The little green at the church gate. The porch of the old schoolhouse. By eleven o'clock, he had decided that constabulary duties had occupied enough of his day. He had been ready to change into rough clothes and spend the afternoon in his garden, when the shout went up that Dorothy Becker was stuck in the graveyard elm. It seemed that she had been trying to rescue Queenie. Judging a life to be at risk, Pinch had ordered that the bell should summon the villagers, but the Vicar overruled him. Tug Macaulay was on the spot, the Reverend said, and Tug Macaulay was all they needed.

So, Pinch had been pushed to the sidelines. The Doctor came, the carter came, and the Verger came with ropes and ladders. Skimpy Cedric Wells, forever acting as Macaulay's fool, dithered and flustered and cried out for his friend to be careful. When Pinch saw that there was nothing for a policeman to do, he withdrew to the churchyard wall and watched the Vicar do the rounds, shaking hands, sharing a word or two, encouraging the ladies to make sure there would be enough tea for everyone afterwards. There was a moment's unease when Doctor Dawes retrieved Dorothy's catapult from the nettle-bed and asked if she had been teasing the pussycat rather than helping. The Doctor confiscated the toy. Pinch stepped forward, but no one made a fuss, so Pinch stepped back again.

Now, the excitement was done with and, at half past five, Pinch promised himself a good couple of hours with his garden before he went indoors. He had much to think about. He had read that Labour Members had laid siege to the House of Lords and he wanted to consider the implications. There was also the matter of itinerant collectors, seeking donations for the striking miners. Should Pinch report their activity? Was it a 'development likely to prejudice the Constitution' or had the Chief Constable's advice been aimed at more weighty dissension? He stretched his back and scratched his head. If he reported the socialists now, so long after their visit, he might be charged with idleness for not submitting the intelligence sooner. A policeman needed to be careful these days. Just last week, a fellow had been fined four pounds for talking to a motor coach driver. "Four pounds," moaned Pinch. "Money I couldn't afford. I wouldn't have thirty bob left for the week."

These were matters best digested while digging.

Arthur Pinch had come to the parish in the Great War. Too old to fight but desperate to serve, he had patrolled the village street waiting for the call, but no summons sounded and Arthur felt that being left behind dogged his reputation. True, during the first years of peace he had saved a toddler's life, but that was one life only; the community had lost seventeen of the twenty-one souls that it had sent soldiering. He had tried to put things right. He had married Peggy, many years his junior, because he thought it was the best way of delivering his promise to her dying mother (although Arthur had since realised that Peggy would have done well to refuse him). Then, three years ago he had convinced the Board to give Miss Carstairs the tenancy of the school cottage during her retirement. He was sure that most villagers could remind him of other ways he had helped. But Pinch still worried that he was far from making up for his non-enlistment, and he was getting on in years. He couldn't expect to last another ten. In less than five, he would be turned out of the Police House and would fall on the parish. He was fifty-six and his wife was thirty. He felt that he was no good to the village and little use to her. Tug Macaulay was a much younger man, a new hero for his neighbours, and Pinch had an ache in his leg.

Worst of all, he could talk to no one about it.

So he went on ruminating as he worked in the garden. Hoeing, tinkering at maintenance and smoking his pipe on the stack of logs behind the shed. Cedric Wells had talked about a hundred thousand women marching on the Commons for peace. What good would that do? Well intentioned, Pinch conceded as he shifted the logs to a more accommodating shape, but can't they see that interfering will do more harm than good?

He repacked his pipe, mumbling, "Perish the man Wells." He shook his box of matches. "A very peaceful man is Cedric Wells."

It was Wells' attitude that irked him more than anything. To see one man fawning over another tested his patience. He didn't like toadies. "They make Sergeants too quickly," he grumbled. "And he drinks women's drinks."

When he noticed that the back garden butt was three quarters full of rainwater, he thought that he might mash some liquid manure for the weekend. He needed half a bushel of animal waste and he had a good pile ready, but he wouldn't start the job without some of the Verger's best pigeon droppings.

"Put Macaulay and his toad out of your mind," he muttered. "Really must."

That evening, Mr and Mrs Pinch sat in their parlour and exchanged hardly a word. He hinted that he had something in mind so, at ten o'clock, when the fire had burned down to a hot bank that would keep the downstairs warm through the small hours, Peggy Pinch closed her detective novel and said, "I think I'll go on up." She knew that her husband would not want her to witness his night-time escapade. As she gathered her things, a draught pushed against the heavy curtain at the door, the standard lamp flickered in the corner of their square room and the last of the coals settled in the little grate.

PC Pinch, comfortable in the opposite armchair, said nothing but inclined his head as she left, and he turned the middle pages of his gardener's journal.

It was one o'clock before Constable Pinch locked his Police House behind him. He collected two hessian sacks from the scullery drain and – dressed in his patched corduroys, turned-down wellingtons and his police macintosh – he unlatched the front gate without a sound. No lights shone from windows up or down The Street but Pinch supposed that he would be spotted by some nosy neighbour or other, so he chose deception in place of straightforwardness and started to plod downhill. The sacks loose at his sides, his fingers curled in his pockets. In recent weeks, he had developed a twinge when walking downhill which he had learned to counter by pushing his left leg forward with each step. It gave his walk a curious tilt.

He knew that Willowby, the clerk, had already cycled home from his evening class in town and Driver David had been out to check the rickety bus parked overnight (Tuesdays and Thursdays only) at the War Memorial. Pinch expected to meet no one else on the road but he didn't correct his direction until the banks of the village ford allowed him to disappear between the backs of two cottages and along the Waddie. (No one could say how the unmade footpath had earned that name.) He was heading for Verger Meggastones' house.

Now, if anyone saw him, they would take him for one of the local characters who walked by night, coming home with a brace of pheasants. But there was no game in Pinch's sacks.

Queen O'Scots trod the same path. They stepped along opposite verges and didn't look at each other but they kept pace and, for fifty yards, it felt that they were walking together. Pinch was sure that Queenie knew all there was to know about the village and she had a way of making herself understood when she had something important to say.

The Hornsbys were still up, drinking beer by lantern light in their little backyard. They were an unsettling pair. Half the village believed in witchcraft and spirits, and Pinch knew that regular séances convened in at least three of the cottages, but Mr and Mrs Hornsby went further. They proclaimed, as certain truth, that demons flew down from the night skies, using the Wishing Stone on Edge Hill as their signalling post before swooping over the village. Not only had they seen the phenomenon but they had caught images on photographic plates which were – and had been for two years – in the hands of the Scientific Office of the Home Department. They told tales of the Professor's Lodge, the grandest house in the village. Tales of girls in white dresses being taken away in a coach with one black horse with sounds of neither hooves nor wheels. Stories of windows in the big house being lit, not from the inside but from the silvery reflections as the alien valkyries delayed their flights and buzzed around this sinister house. Shadows of The Lodge, said the Hornsbys, fell in ways no honest shadow could fall.

Hornsby was on his feet. "Who's that, you reckon?"

"No one," Mrs Hornsby decided, giving her husband's query little or no thought.

Pinch waited for the moment when the clouds masked the moon (and, yes, the crooked shadow of the Professor's home did drop like a curtain across the cottages in a curious way). But if the cat wasn't bothered, neither was Pinch, so the pair trudged on. He had already decided to put it about that Poacher Baines had been seen in the neighbourhood. After tonight, the Hornsbys would be eager to add to that rumour.

He was careful as he passed Miss Edie's cottage. All the world knew that she slept with a hand bell beneath her bed in case of burglars. Good Heavens, Pinch didn't want to explain causing that sort of alarm. Then he paid special attention at the back of the Becker's modest home. Word was that Ruby was stealing from her husband's pockets and Pinch had a notion that the man might want to teach her a lesson. Their children were the naughtiest in the village; the Willowbys, next door, were the best behaved. And, on the opposite side of the footpath, poor Widow Jenner was in the last days of a pregnancy. But, at nearly two in the morning, there was no sound from one place or the others.

Queen O'Scots stopped in mid-step, her paw raised, her head cocked. Just a second later, Pinch looked over his shoulder and saw that the cat had hidden herself in the clumps of long grass. He waited. Rustles and a slap, and the schoolma'am's cat had caught her supper.

A bird flew from one tree to another, the winged shape turning bigger and blacker as it crossed the face of the moon. Further up – at the very top of the village hill – another bird squawked in the branches and Pinch had to remind himself that he would have nothing to do with omens.

He felt in his pocket for his pipe but knew that he shouldn't smoke until the job was done.

Not thirty yards from the Verger's garden, Pinch pressed himself against an oak tree. The grey shapes of the church reached above him. Pinch needed to be sure that no one was about. He had lived in the village for ten years and he knew that it wasn't uncommon for a troubled parishioner to seek peace in the church after hours. Also, a tramp called Gregory had been seen in the neighbouring village and, if he kept to his well-tried calendar, he was due to make the churchyard his home for five or six nights before moving on.

Pinch lodged himself comfortably against the trunk and resolved to keep motionless for ten minutes – twenty minutes or even longer

– before venturing through the Verger's ramshackle hedge. Queen O'Scots, back with him, wanted to join in the observations. She found an overhanging branch and stretched herself into a perfect shape of camouflage, but Pinch sensed that she wasn't at ease. She inched forward, then arched her back and kept her head low. It was as if the cat had found something she could either watch or hear, but she could neither do both nor decide which. The night birds were still. Yes, they saw that the cat was irritable and that would have been enough to silence them, but everything above ground was like a frozen, expectant image. (Like those few seconds before the whistle blew in the trenches, Pinch supposed.)

Pinch waited.

Halfway down the lane, a woman in slippers walked to her outside lavatory. A wayward pet toppled crates in the untidy yard of the Red Lion. St Stephen's clock wanted to chime half past two but the mechanism was known to be broken; the minute hand slapped twice, noisily, against the thirtieth dash before breaking through and starting its upward progress.

Then he heard a rustling in the long grass in the corner of the graveyard. A burrowing, a thrashing but the sounds were excited rather than desperate. This wasn't a fox or fowl breaking through the undergrowth, or a bedraggled vagrant making his bed for the night. Something indulgent was going on. 'These are greedy noises,' thought Constable Pinch.

He hid the sacks in an exposed root of the oak, then slid across the ditch. Carefully, he edged forward; one step, then another and another until he plainly heard the sighs of a woman in the middle of lovemaking. He kept perfectly still and stared hard.

Mollie Sweatman was being serviced by strongman Macaulay, out at night from his lodgings in Old School Cottage.

Pinch wanted a better look. Mollie was always cocky and brash, a dozen years older than the thrilling new woodworker, and Pinch knew that if he could glimpse whatever she was showing, the pictures would stay in his head forever. He had often imagined the extra weight that this rude and loud woman carried in her saddlebags and, at least once in every week, he caught himself smiling at a fancy of how her oversized breasts might flop if she let them free. How white they'd be! My God, tonight – tonight! – he might catch her flagrantly indecent. If only he could gain another twenty yards. What if he could make it to the bank of old headstones where the bones of French prisoners lay buried? He would have the best view from there. His neck itched in his collar. 'Mollie Sweatman, as bare as she was born,' he repeated, over and over, in his head. 'Mollie Sweatman bare!' Pinch had to bite his lip to stop himself swooning.

But before the policeman could make a proper study, he realised that he wasn't the only spectator. A pair of white eyes glistened from the other side of the stage. The figure was lying face down in the grass. The angle of the moonlight and the shadow of the church tower weren't right for Pinch to identify his fellow observer; he couldn't even make out the shape of his face. Cedric Wells? Who else would follow Tug Macaulay and Mollie Sweatman in the middle of the night?

Pinch was frustrated but he knew that he needed to withdraw. He needed a ready excuse for being here, and he would much rather admit to being a poacher of pigeon droppings than a Peeping Tom.

But then, retreat was compromised.

From the drifting mist of night-time, came the slapping of flat soled shoes on mud. Hair askew and hands working to keep up speed and a shallow panting made giggly by the issue of words that no one was meant to hear, little Edie Snag was out of bed and running around the village.

Pinch pushed himself against the tree roots.

"Miss Carstairs knows all about it," Edie was explaining to herself. "Schoolmistress knows best. Knows better than any Vicar. Miss Carstairs knows it and all about it and she'll tell the truth in the morning."

Pinch crawled backwards, conscious of the noise his belly was making, unavoidably, on the rough grass. He had wanted to keep his raid on the Verger's garden secret, but now he would find reassurance from gossip: 'Aye, our Bobby was out and about last night but he was only pinching pigeon muck, nothing more than that.' The village would believe it and smile at the rivalry between

11

its two best gardeners. But he needed to extricate himself from the graveyard without being seen.

He bent his neck back and saw plump Mollie sitting up, topless and white in the moonshine but how could Pinch relish the sight when he was stuck in No Man's Land, inching his way back to the friendly trenches? What snipers were in the dark trees above him? 'Where are you now, Queenie?' he wanted to whisper. 'For God's sake, help me to safety.' His face was wet, his fingers dirty, his feet cold in their boots. He had almost reached the ditch of brambles when he heard Mollie's harshly crowed thrill, "Oh, if she could see us now, that prim-arsed Pinch-woman. She'd see you're twice the size of her husband."

The words froze in Arthur Pinch's brain.

"Peggy Pinch!" Mollie shouted, not caring who heard. "The prim-arse of the Wishing Pool!"

Animal waste needed to soak for two days to produce good liquid manure. If it was to be used as one treatment the sack could be squeezed, giving the potion extra strength, but if it was used one slurp at a time, dung and rainwater could be added in alternate portions and the mix would keep going for a season. Pinch made very good manure but the Verger's was better because he lived at the top of the hill and, each day, could collect pigeon droppings from the outside walls of the church. Pigeon droppings gave it excellence.

Meggastones kept the mess in the dirty corner of his garden, between the potting shed and an ancient hedge. The hedge provided good cover for Pinch. He progressed stealthily along the edge of the garden, then knelt in the coarse grass and laid his two sacks – one empty, one full – beside the water butt. He put his nose beneath the wooden lid and, although the stink brought him up, he knew it smelled good.

"Prim Arse?" he whispered. Well, if the women called her that, she had only herself to blame. Peggy was quiet and looked smug; she would never chat like the others did. Smug? No, something showier than that. Tscht, he couldn't think of the word.

He sunk his hands into the water and withdrew the dripping hessian. He collected fistfuls of dung and laid it in the empty sack, then tipped his muck into the Verger's sack, which he topped up with some of the quality stuff. Then he wrapped the stolen mess in his own sacks and tied it off. It was a straightforward job but the policeman took his time. He wouldn't be spotted between the shed and the hedge, but his coming and going in the Waddie needed care.

He pushed his way, backwards, through the hedge (after all, it was only fair to leave the Verger some clues that his garden had been disturbed).

"Leary," he muttered. "That's the word. My wife's a leary one." Peggy had lived in the village all her life. She had shared the schoolroom with girls who were now gossipy wives, and they didn't forget the tidy, well dressed girl who kept herself to herself and was too clever by far. Miss Mullens of the Red Lion always said that the best time of her schooldays was the morning when Peggy got the stick in front of all the children.

> *Peggy, oh Peggy, her face like a piggy*
> *Cried 'Oink oink,' at the taste o' old twiggy.*

A childish nonsense rhyme, but it was still commonplace behind Peggy's back.

"All the same," he said as he dragged himself from the hedge. "Strange, that dollopy Mollie should call my wife's name in her moments of passion."

As he trod his first steps on the footpath, he was brought up by the silent figure of the young Dorothy Becker, caught in a shift of moonlight. She didn't say a word, she didn't move and Pinch had to study the indistinct lines of her shape to be sure that he wasn't facing a ghost. Standing calmly in her belted raincoat, pigtails in ribbons, and shiny sandals, this wasn't the picture of a girl who had stepped out of home at a moment's thought. This was a regular truant. "You get yourself to bed, Dorothy Becker, before I knock up your father and tell tales on you. Go on, be off!"

13

Her white eyes were her clearest feature. They didn't flinch as she turned, almost politely, and stepped towards home.

It seemed that half the village was out of doors that night and, Pinch guessed, the Becker girl had seen most of the goings-on.

CHAPTER TWO

The Murder of Cedric Wells

Cedric Wells was murdered at half past eleven, the next morning. The tragedy meant that most of the village would go without lunch, infants would be kept at the church kindergarten until their grown-ups arrived, and Pinch would postpone another afternoon's gardening.

The morning had already been disrupted. The men had been at Foyle's Bridge since the small hours, repairing damage caused by an overturned hay-cart. The accident slowed the stream, which helped the work, but it also flooded a nearby pond and, by first light, the road between village and town was impassable. When the young and excited scouts, dispatched to Holt's Crossing, came back with news that the way was clear through neighbouring villages, Driver David stepped up to the mark and declared that his thrice weekly bus service would run by the round-about route. But the villagers knew there would be no first post and no newspapers to read.

No one grumbled about the interruptions. Indeed, being out of touch with national affairs felt like a day off. Men and women stepped about the village street in something of a holiday mood. Some interested parties wondered if the choir might give an impromptu recital in the church that afternoon but the Vicar was new and no one went forward with the proposal.

No newspapers was a trouble for Pinch. He was still worried about the travelling socialists. Six weeks ago, he had received an unminuted visit from a Force Superintendent, delivering instructions that Pinch was to privately report any active dissension against the government. Of course, Pinch was aware that people were concerned about working class unrest but he couldn't understand why his quiet, rural patch should be singled out for this attention. But he'd keep an eye out, he'd said. He had given little attention to the townies, collecting for miners' families. But now he had picked up word of the disorder in Parliament, when Labour Members had besieged the House of Lords, and he wondered what he ought to do about the charity volunteers. Should he go as far as naming those households that had given generously? Pinch was no good at deciding these matters on his own. Until recently he would have talked with the old Vicar and, confident that the conversation was private, he would have drawn on clerical advice. But this new Vicar was untested, and they didn't get on. He had rather counted on reading the newspaper report of the Westminster incident before making up his mind what to do. But an upturned hay-cart had got in the way of that.

He stood at the top of The Street, itching to smoke his pipe but clasping his hands behind his back. The village was busy. Customers popped in and out of the Post Office, work progressed on St Stephen's roof and old Berkeley was making deliveries from his barrow in Wretched Lane. The Vicar's maid and Miss Carstairs, the retired schoolma'am, had been standing at the War Memorial for forty-five minutes. They had boarded the ramshackle omnibus, in spite of David's warning of a long journey to town, but no sooner were they settled in their seats than a failed motor brought them off again. Driver David couldn't get it going.

Nearby, Dr Dawes had parked his two seater motorcar on the grass verge, close to the twitchel that led to Widow Jenner's hovel. The Vicar's daily help and the retired teacher were joined by Martha Hornsby and, together, the women were marking the length of the Doctor's visit. Mrs Jenner was near her time and too long a visit could be a worrying sign. Dorothy Becker was trying to convince the Willowby child to play a practical joke while the Doctor was away from his car. Peggy stood close enough for them to know she was keeping an eye on them.

At a quarter to ten, realising that two outstretched legs were all they were going to see of him, the three women left David beneath the engine and went their different ways. The Vicar's maid said that she could usefully spend an hour in the kitchen garden and Mrs Hornsby wanted to take a picnic to the Wishing Stone. Miss Carstairs, who had promised to gather shopping for other households, spent twenty minutes in the Post Office, writing her renewed plans on separate scraps of paper so that the Postmistress could hand them out as the housewives came into the shop.

Then, as she was making her way back to her cottage, she was caught by Doctor Dawes who pressed his offer of a lift.

"And how is Mrs Jenner?" asked the old schoolma'am.

"Preparing well, preparing well. It will be another two weeks. Now, come, Miss Carstairs, you need to go to town and you'll enjoy a jolly in the motor. Exhilarating, I promise you."

Miss Carstairs hesitated; she had gained a large plate of the Postmistress's scones and wanted to set them out so that they wouldn't go doughy. (Everyone knew that the Postmistress's cooking was best eaten promptly.)

"I'll take care of them," piped up Peggy Pinch.

"Oh, would you, dear? But my place, not yours. They'll keep nicely on the kitchen table covered with light muslin, but you'll need to leave the window on the third notch. Please, it is important."

"Don't worry."

Peggy had already taken charge of the plate and Miss Carstairs was being installed in the passenger seat of Dawes' new motorcar. When the Doctor was ready for the off, the rural peace was disturbed by bellowing hoots as a steam-driven dray clanked and wheezed its way from the top of The Street. Nobody had expected traffic, today of all days. Immediately, Dorothy Becker and her two friends were in the middle of the road, scampering about the wagon's wheels like puppy dogs eager to play. The drayman always came with button biscuits in stout paper bags with District Bank printed on the face.

"Hey, Mister! Hey Mister!"

"That child," grumbled the Doctor. "Why can't she behave? She'll do the Willowby girl a bad turn, mark my words." Then he remembered that he had taken the girl's toy but hadn't told the mother. Instinctively, he felt the inside pocket of his jacket. Then he recalled that he had put the catapult away for safekeeping.

With one great expulsion of air, the dray came to a stop. Dawes knew that the carter had no hope of shunting into the inn's yard, so he pulled his car to the verge and started pulling – backwards and forwards, backwards and forwards – until he was able to steer around the obstacle.

Miss Carstairs took advantage of the delay to lean out of the door and call, "Don't wake Mr Macaulay. He hardly got any rest last night, I know. He'll sleep through till two or three."

Peggy was waving. "Don't worry. I'll see to things." She thought that the Carstairs lodger was far more likely to be woken by the circus sounds of the dray than her own discreet entry to the back kitchen. "See you before tea time!"

The car growled away, the Doctor chattering loudly and his uncomfortable passenger trying to make the best of things.

Constable Pinch watched the commotion from the church gate at the top of the hill while Verger Meggastones, wanting to keep an eye on the parish's peculiar Professor, stayed hidden in the long garden of his cottage. Ruby Becker sat on her backdoor step, weeping as she nursed her bruised cheek. Miss Mullens drank tea with young Alice, her pub cleaner. (Alice and her young man were virtually engaged, she said.) Mrs Willowby was putting on her coat and pictured her husband at work in an office in town and her children playing nicely in the village brook. (She didn't know that son and daughter had separated.) The schoolma'am's cat, who habitually spent her mornings indoors, was curled on the staircase window ledge, her eyes closed but still awake.

Peggy was in a careless mood as she carried the plate of scones through Miss Carstairs' side door. She called 'Good afternoon,' just loud enough to excuse herself, but she kept her voice low because she didn't want to wake the lodger. The kitchen had the personal touch of a retired lady with high standards and many memories, but it looked little worked. Miss Carstairs kept house for herself and her lodger, made sure that the Becker child had a good breakfast and, until recently, she had cooked an extra lunch, three days a week, which she carried across to Bulpit Cottage. Not to mention the expectations of the Queen O'Scots. Yet there was so little evidence of work in this kitchen that she was able to keep a vase of fresh flowers on the table and a collage of pressed leaves at the window. Not for the first time, Peggy pictured the elderly woman delicately sipping tea from an expensive cup, with the window open so that she could pretend the birds weren't calling to each other but singing to her. Peggy was sure that such solitude was beyond any married woman; she couldn't imagine sitting in the kitchen of the Police House without knowing where Pinch was or if he was going to walk in on her.

She set the tray on the kitchen table and, almost dutifully (for, although Clemency Carstairs no longer taught, she would always be Peggy's schoolmistress) she spaced the scones across two plates and covered them loosely with the white cloth. She opened the window to the third notch. Then, when she should have withdrawn, she stood and gazed at the parlour door. She wanted to find other things to do. She washed her hands. She wiped the rim of the sink. She checked the taps. Then she leaned her back against the cupboard, put her hands over her tummy and twiddled her thumbs.

Macaulay was asleep, Miss Carstairs was in town and no one would discover whatever Peggy did in the cottage that morning.

Already, she was feeling the heat of being alone in the house with him. Just thinking about him, upstairs in bed, should have been naughty enough, but curiosity tugged at her. It wanted to lead her by the nose, passing over things that she hadn't properly thought about, deciding things without giving her chance to argue. She felt her cheeks blush. She shook her head. She sat down, put her elbows on the table and hid her face in her hands.

She should leave. She no longer had any business here. But the more she hesitated, the more she heard Mollie Sweatman's teasing. "You're married now, Peggy, and you'll never know if he's up to strength." That whisper in the church porch on her wedding day was like Ariadne's Thread, drawing her back to their night at the Wishing Pool.

She knocked politely on the door and stepped into the front

room. Miss Carstairs' needles and wool had been put away, her weekly journal was stowed beneath the armchair cushion and the little fire had been allowed to burn down. Miss Carstairs didn't expect to be home before tea time.

Nothing was out of place in this room and only the tick-tock of the wall clock policed what went on. Carrying her heels, Peggy stepped lightly across the polished floorboards and unlatched the door to the staircase.

"Coo-ee?" But her words were too soft to be a serious enquiry.

She put one hand on the banister post and the toe of one shoe on the first stair.

Queen O'Scots emerged from a landing alcove and stood at the stairhead. Like Peggy, she paused with one foot forward. They both knew that the cat wasn't allowed at the top of the stairs and that Peggy had no business at the bottom. Miss Carstairs wouldn't have been surprised to find a neighbour in her kitchen and she would have accepted a modest excuse for being found in the parlour, but how could Peggy explain being upstairs (if upstairs was where she would go)?

Years before, when the schoolmistress had caught Peggy out of bounds, the child had suffered such a telling off that she promised never to trespass again. Now, the wrong of breaking that promise worried her more than the wrong of climbing the little staircase. Peggy and the cat stayed still and watched each other.

For days to come she would ask herself how long was she in the cottage. It would grow into the most important question about the murder of Cedric Wells. But Peggy would never be able to say for sure. It felt as if she and Queenie were face to face for half an hour, but it couldn't have been that long.

In The Street, the innkeeper was paying-off the drayman and, racing downhill, the Willowby lad was ringing his bicycle bell as he steered towards the village ford. The gulley, alongside Miss Carstairs garden path, was rushed through with water as Martha Hornsby tipped her washing.

Halfway up the stairs, Peggy sat down and rested her elbows on her knees. She needed to get the memory out of her head.

Four years ago, when her mother and father had been dead for two years, when she knew Pinch but hadn't married him, when she was feeling that she had no choice in life but to play the cards that had been dealt to her, Peggy had watched the village team play on a cricket ground, eight miles from home. She got separated from her neighbours and had to walk home alone. It was already dark when she heard laughter and squeals coming from the banks of the Wishing Pool. At first, she thought that some of the villagers were playing at witchcraft but as she got nearer to the water's edge, she saw only one woman making all the noise. Dollopy Mollie Sweatman was splashing about with her clothes off. She tried to entice Peggy to join in, teasing her for prudishness. It wasn't long before the woman's malice got the better of her tongue. "You'll be thirty, Peggy Prim-Arse, and you won't have seen what a man's got for you. You won't know what's wee and what's large. Would you buy a lump of meat without seeing what else is on the slab?" Coarse and horrible and enough to make Peggy hurry along home. But the taunt had never been put down. It lived on in Mollie's eyes and grins, and the curious expression of her lips when only Peggy could see and, although the words were weary in the back of Peggy's mind, they wouldn't be put to bed.

Peggy knew that if she challenged her conscience, her conscience would lose, so she asked no further questions of herself. She rose from the step of indecision and continued up the stairs. Later, she would want to say that she didn't know properly what she was doing.

At the top, Queenie walked in a figure of eight between her legs, brushing them softly, lightly, friendly; then the cat leapt onto the ledge of the little round window overlooking the back gardens of The Street.

Peggy didn't knock. She curled her fingers around the doorknob and, more carefully than any burglar, turned it in her hand. No one made a sound.

She pushed. Then, when the door was ajar, leaned forward to see inside.

He was sleeping noisily, but otherwise he was dead to the world. The blankets had slipped to the floor and the sheets had twisted around his legs so that his bronzed, savage back was bare. She stepped into the room, stood at the corner of the bed and stared at him. She knew that if she passed from this side of the bed to the other, she would see him exposed.

Until that morning, Arthur Pinch was the only man she had seen. The first time, she had been anxious that there might be more of him than she could imagine but, when it was revealed, it looked small and funny. Pinch. It seemed so properly named. Pinch's Pinch. But a man like Tug Macaulay could only be a proper size and shape; if he was a disappointment, then all men must be the same.

Blood pulsed at her temples and neck, and her eyes were smarting. She couldn't avert her stare as, inch by inch, more of his body came into view. She caught her breath and, at that last moment of innocent curiosity, she kept her feet together and leaned forward to look.

A scream of pain startled her. She shot back against the bedroom wall as she turned and stumbled onto the landing. Queen O'Scots, in full flight, jumped on her back and, instinctively going for height against any unknown threat, she leapt from the bedroom carpet to the bed to the top of the wardrobe. Peggy rushed down the stairs, two and three at a time, knocking her shoulders and hips and all-but turning her ankles. She was through the kitchen and at the back door before she realised that she'd heard no sound of Macaulay getting out of bed.

Outside, she leaned heavily against the brick wall. Who had seen her? Had she said anything that others could have heard? Her knees were weak and she felt ready to turn in on herself but, when her vision cleared, she saw that Mollie was in The Street, wailing as loud as she could as she knelt beside Cedric Wells' collapsed body. Driver David was squatting at the casualty's feet, doing nothing. Blood was on his shirt, Mollie's hands were alive with it and heavy drips were forming a soggy patch beneath Cedric's lifeless skull.

Pinch quick marched from the Police House. "Get away. Keep clear," he called in the familiar tone that usually brought calm to everything. As he reached the gathering, he heard Cedric's strangled gasp. "Give him some air," he ordered. "Come on now, loosen his collar."

Everyone knew that Cedric's utterance had been no more than his death rattle but still the fingers worked at his knotted tie, the collar stud and buttons of his shirt. Knuckles and nails got in one another's way. Other people were crying now, not just Mollie.

Then Mollie's wailing spiralled into a hysterical shriek. She rocked back on her heels, shaking her head and scratching at her tear soaked cheeks.

Newcomers stayed standing.

"My God, our Cedric isn't at all!" said Ruby Becker.

"My God!" said Miss Mullens from the Red Lion.

Alice the cleaner leaned forward, twisting a duster between her hands. "The Devil, he is!"

Ruby Becker was reaching a red-faced crescendo. "He isn't! Isn't Cedric at all! No!

Three women cried in unison: "Our Cedric Wells is a woman!"

Pinch judged that enforcing discipline was the best way of keeping the peace. "Everyone, quiet! Peggy, a blanket please for Cedric Wells."

But Peggy was hemmed in by the gathering women.

"A woman? A woman all this time?"

"And right in the middle of us?"

"Look at her! Look at her!" Mollie shouted, running on the spot and pointing at the evidence.

Then Doctor Dawes arrived and the Red Sea parted. His pressed two fingers against the dead woman's neck and confirmed sombrely, "Oh, God, I feared this might happen. One blanket will do, I'm afraid, for the sake of compassion."

Pinch nodded. "Killed by a stone, I'd say. Thrown from high up."

"I heard someone rushing from the top of Old School Cottage," Mollie tried to say; her hysterics would only allow words in short puffs. "Near as broke the staircase."

"Pinch, please. Allow her some privacy," said the Doctor but no one took any notice. "Please, give her some space, some air."

"From the top, you say?" Pinch looked at the bedroom window of Old School Cottage. "Well, that can only be one man."

"Aye, and he was promising such to our Mr Wells," someone

shouted from the back. "Didn't we all hear it? He was sick of his attentions, didn't he say it? Sick and tired. That's what he said."

"I was only in there for a couple of minutes, setting out a tray of scones," said Peggy, although she hadn't been asked. When no one responded (they were too busy trying to look at the revealed nature of Cedric's true gender) she added, "Then I walked around the flowerbeds at the back."

Pinch withdrew from the body and turned to the crowd. "All right, every one. Get away from here. I shall make an arrest at once. Doctor, if you'll take Driver Davy and ready yourselves on the path in case of trouble"

Like characters on a stage, and with hardly a word, the two men stood sentry at the gate and the women assembled in a single line on the far side of the road. Three of the women held hands. Peggy wanted to fold her arms across her tummy. She felt queasy, confused and listless and, after fidgeting, stayed with her arms limp at her sides. The body was left, covered up and abandoned, so that when Jones' horse and cart clip-clopped through the scene, the farmer thought the bundle needed picking up and he would have stopped if the Doctor hadn't waved him on.

Macaulay didn't resist arrest. The spectators caught only a glimpse of him but each noted that he looked as erect and broad-shouldered as ever. The Doctor and driver fell in as the escort and Pinch led the detachment down the back garden path, along the rough Waddie and up from the ford. A roundabout route, but within five minutes the suspect was locked in the little cell at the back of the Police House.

The landlady and Ruby remained to guard the body. Peggy started to drift home but was soon caught by Mollie Sweatman.

"What were you doing all that time?" Mollie asked, "with Miss Carstairs not being there?"

Peggy's heart started to race again. "I was popping in some scones, that's all."

"No, it's not. It's not all at all. Half an hour, as good as, you were in there. And you came squiggling out the back like a naughty schoolgirl."

"Mollie, please."

The tears were old on Mollie's cheeks but the eyes that had hardly believed the truth about Cedric Wells, sparkled at the prospect of being one-up on Peggy Pinch. Mollie's face always looks fatter when she's being a bitch, Peggy thought.

"Well, just you bear in mind," Mollie said, tasting each word. "Bear in mind, Cedric Wells has been murdered, battered on the back of the head by one who meant it and you, Peggy Prim-Arse, don't want people to know what you were up to when all this was done."

CHAPTER THREE

Pinch's Parlour

Two hours later and the evening was cold. Stillness lay like a blanket over the village, so that neither leaves nor grass disturbed in the ditches and not one bird bothered the hedgerows. Greater than the chill and the stillness was a forbidding silence that not only kept faces from the windows but pushed the villagers to sit indoors with their backs to the lanes. Tomorrow, they would touch each other, they would seek and offer brief words of comfort, and the busy-bodies might give tongue to the malicious thoughts in people's minds. But not tonight. Tonight, the village had lost its breath. The more spiritual brows worried that the suffocating air was a sign that Wells' soul hadn't been able to rise up from the place. For years, a woman had lived in their midst as a man and now murder had been done. Tonight, each fact made the other unmentionable. The village turned its face away in shame.

Then, just two or three signs of life beyond the closed front doors. Jones brought his horse and cart to the triangle of green at the top of The Street. They rested, too nervous to progress down the road between the houses. Jones relaxed the rein so that the horse could take him wherever the horse wanted to go. They stepped around the church green, turned awkwardly at the gate and, a few minutes later, were nowhere to be seen. Miss Mullens drew the inside bolts on the pub doors, not expecting customers that evening, and at a quarter to seven, the Vicar told the organist to go home; there would be no congregation for evensong. Queens O'Scots, a black cat, walked silently over the ground where the body had

26

fallen and stationed herself at the Police House gate. She heard the Doctor leave by the side door of the surgery, fifty yards down the road. She heard him pass along his garden path and open and close his rattling wrought iron gate.

Harry Dawes wore a weary tweed suit with stretched elbows and pockets, and old brown brogues which he always kept polished and studded. He was short, with bushy hair over the ears of an otherwise bald head, a nose that allowed no air to get to his titchy moustache and a bottom that weighed too much for his legs. He kept his reading glasses half in the top pocket of the jacket, with his stethoscope hanging out of his left hand pocket and two handkerchiefs bulging in the other. He jingled copper coins in one side of his trousers, and a couple of silver coins and his third best penknife opposite. From the inside of his jacket, he could produce cigarettes in a gunmetal case, two fountains pens (one with green ink) and a wallet of newspaper (and other) cuttings. All these accoutrements made him look like a bumbling conjurer who had been unable to tuck away the tricks of his trade. It was an apt caricature; Dawes would have made an excellent clown in the village revue.

But this evening he didn't hum or pom-pom to himself as he approached the Police House. There was much that he would be asked to explain; he wondered what he could keep back and, already, how he could make the best of the changed circumstances.

As the Doctor's fingers reached for the gate, Queenie withdrew to the hedgebottom. She had learned to be wary of this man's toecaps.

Peggy opened the door before he had time to knock and she guided him into the little parlour. Then she left by the front door, walked down the side path and re-entered the kitchen by the back door so that she didn't interrupt the gentlemen.

Opposite, Clemency Carstairs considered herself to be Peggy's best friend. She wrapped a shawl around her shoulders, folded a white apron over one arm, collected the dish of tarts from her windowsill and managed to keep it all in place as she hurried across The Street. She had seen the Chief Constable's man arrive an hour ago. Now the Doctor wanted to hear Pinch's story and she wouldn't be surprised if the Vicar turned up before long. Poor Peggy, with so much on her mind, would welcome another pair of hands.

"Who's the policeman?" she asked as she entered the back of the Police House.

Peggy was standing in the middle of the kitchen, doing nothing.

"A Superintendent from Headquarters, not our usual man. It's as if our Inspector and Sergeant have been told to stay away. It feels horrible out there," she added quietly. "I think our peculiar Professor is weeping at the wayside. He takes any death very sensitively."

Miss Carstairs was already arranging things. "Come on, then, Peggy. Let's get to work. You've given them tea?"

"As soon as he arrived." She looked around her kitchen. "I was just thinking of taking a cup in for Doctor Dawes."

"Lay for a fresh pot." She folded her shawl over a breakfast chair and knotted the apron strings behind her back. "Come on, my girl, no point in worrying more than you have to."

Then, without further words, the women decided that tea and cakes could wait. They went to the closed door of the parlour, and listened.

"You did well, Pinch," the Superintendent was saying. "Arresting Macaulay at the first opportunity."

"I thought it best." Pinch spoke in a deep chomping voice; he always did when he wasn't sure about things. "The village will have so much to think about that it seemed kindly to close one door promptly. The stories of our disguised woman will be wild enough without being fuelled by doubts and speculation."

The Superintendent agreed. "We have a solid case against the scoundrel, all thanks to you."

Peggy shook her head but Miss Carstairs pressed her lips to keep quiet.

"What did he say to you?" the Superintendent asked.

Pinch didn't need to refer to his notes. "He said, 'I never did like the cuss' and he had to stop him. He didn't attempt to deny it."

Peggy clutched Miss Carstairs' arm. "No, no," she whispered.

"Why's he saying that? Mr Macaulay wouldn't have said anything of the sort."

Miss Carstairs took her hand and led her away from the door. "Here are the tarts from Postmistress Mary, and I've brought some of my own jam."

"But you don't understand, Miss Carstairs. Pinch is saying things that can't possibly be true."

"Now, come on, you'll have some of your lovely apricot treat left, I'm sure."

Peggy went on shaking her head. "I can't believe it. Cedric Wells was a woman?"

Miss Carstairs stepped back from the table and turned to Peggy's Welsh dresser. "Her real name was Cedar," she said quietly. "Wells was her maiden name."

"You knew all along?" Peggy mouthed. She watched the old woman turn pale. In one moment, everything about Clemency Carstairs seemed to go limp.

The schoolma'am gave up her attempts to keep her friend busy. Avoiding Peggy's eyes, she set about preparing a tea for the gentlemen and when she looked over her shoulder, Peggy was sitting with the crochet shawl around her and she was playing with the cotton tassels. "Of all the women in the village," Miss Carstairs confessed, "I probably had the best motive to kill Cedar. She was married to an old friend, a dear friend. Because he was married to her, we could allow nothing to come of our friendship. I often think that Cedar came to our parish to taunt me."

Peggy did not say anything. She couldn't think of any gentleman in her old schoolteacher's life. Then, she remembered, from years ago, looking through the window of School Cottage and catching an image of two people sharing a late night supper. "The school inspector?" she sighed, more to herself than her friend.

"Please, Peg. You must tell no one."

"But that was a lifetime away. Before the War. I was a child."

As a silence lay between them, they heard the padded sounds of the men talking in the next room.

"Please, Peggy."

29

"Who else knew?"

Miss Carstairs was patting jam onto a saucer and keeping an eye on the apricot butter warming on the range.

"About Cedar, you mean? I'm sure that Doctor Dawes was aware of her true identity. I think he as good as told me, on one occasion. And I wonder if the Vicar's wife knows something."

"But she hasn't been seen in the village," said Peggy, puzzled, knowing that she was being told too much to make sense of.

"Our Postmistress Mary says that there might be a secret here that she's frightened of. That's why she's reluctant to move into the Vicarage."

Peggy shook her head. "I don't know what's going on. Miss Carstairs, I hate it."

"Yet, Miss Mullens has heard that the Vicar's father-in-law has suffered a stroke and his wife has stayed behind to nurse him."

Peggy, hardly listening, was ready to cry. "I can't understand any of it."

Their talk gave way to the clank and clatter of Thurrock's steam traction engine as it made its ungainly progress from the top of the village to the ford. As it passed the Police House, lights flickered, the cooking range groaned on its clawed feet and things in the kitchen rattled. Murder or no murder, Foyle's Bridge still needed righting.

When quiet returned, the women could hear the words of the men in the next room.

"I need to explain," the Doctor was saying. "I have known that Cedric Wells was a woman for more than a year. She was a regular patient, you understand. She was a slave to inflamed glands, I'm sorry to say. Hardly ever free of them."

"She was hit by a stone, you've said?" asked the Superintendent.

"Well, more than hit. I have seen such injuries only twice before in my career. Both times, a catapult was to blame."

At the scullery table, Miss Carstairs and Peggy looked at each other. "Ruby Becker's girl?" whispered the old schoolma'am. Peggy gave no reaction; she was setting cups and saucers on a tea tray. Miss Carstairs went back to smoothing her homemade jam on half a dozen tarts,

"But please, no hurried conclusions." The women pictured the Doctor, holding one hand in the air as the other brushed unruly spiders of hair from his ears. "The only catapult I've known in the village is safely locked in the top drawer of my surgery desk. I confiscated it from young Dorothy Becker on the night of the rescue."

Peggy opened the parlour door and stretched out a hand so that Miss Carstairs could enter with the tea trolley. "We're all very tired," she said softly to Peggy.

"That looks like a fine feast, ladies, but I must be off!" The Superintendent looked sharp in his brushed, pressed uniform. A kick of his long legs propelled him to his feet. "Well, the matter has been handed over to the detective branch," he said. "As you say, Doctor, we mustn't rush to conclusions." He was looking around for his baton and gloves; his cap was already tucked beneath his arm. "Keep your journal up to date, Pinch. All registers and ledgers." He slapped the accoutrements to his side. "I would value a report about your travelling Labourites. I quite understand why you didn't want to cause alarm initially, but all these matters need to be considered in the new light of murder."

The Superintendent dipped his head politely towards the two ladies and shook hands with the Doctor. "Makes you wonder, would things have been different if the coach had been working."

It was obvious that the Doctor meant to stay behind. Now that the superior officer had gone, he took the commanding position on the hearthrug and tapped his pockets as if he were searching for something. Pinch recognised the nervous habit; Dawes felt uncomfortable about something.

"Pinch," he began and hesitated. If he was waiting for some encouragement, Pinch resolved not to oblige. "Pinch, I want Miss Carstairs to hear what I say. I'm sure she will agree with my sentiments."

The look on her husband's face left Peggy in no doubt that she was allowed to stay in the room only because she was with the old schoolmistress. She busied herself at the trolley as Miss Carstairs handed selections to the men; there was no thought that the women would share the tea.

"Our new Reverend must be brought into this," said the Doctor. "We cannot have a murder when the village Bobby isn't talking to its Vicar. It won't do."

Pinch said nothing.

"The chap has made a faux pas, recommending that the parish library should move from Edie Snag's cottage to the old Vestry but, surely, he didn't know how people would feel about that. Yes, he countermanded your order that the alarm should be rung but, as soon as he realised the tradition of the bell, he told the Verger to proceed. It cannot be, Pinch; he cannot be left in the cold. The village needs its Vicar at a time like this."

The Constable didn't stir in his chair. His chin stayed resting on a curled hand. His feet were lodged with crossed ankles.

"Mark my words, Pinch," Dawes added irritably. "Tomorrow The Street and Wretched Lane will be full of trippers with their cheap cameras and the Red Lion with be packed with penny paper men."

The Doctor departed within half an hour but Miss Carstairs, who had said nothing to support Dawes' arguments, stayed until the cutlery was washed and polished and the crockery had been safely stowed on the shelves. Peggy walked with her to the front gate.

"This death will bring trouble to our village, Peg." Queen O' Scots was waiting on the other side of the road. "Before the matter's settled, our lives will have changed and many of us will walk with different looks on our faces. The Beckers, the Hornsbys, you, me and those in the Vicarage. We'll never be the same".

After supper, Peggy took up her evening mending and Pinch sat at their front window. His old hide armchair was placed so that, with hardly a movement of his neck, he could watch things up The Street or things in his sittingroom. His pipe and tobacco were on the arm but he seemed to want nothing to do with them.

Peggy knew that it was a mistake to interrupt him in his garden or when he was reading or working at his jigsaw or when, with fine brushes, he was intricately dusting the magnificent table top locomotive called Black Prince. But she had also learned to recognise those moods when her husband wasn't comfortable with his thoughts and some talk might be a welcome respite. Wanting to prompt rather than initiate a conversation, she pretended to think aloud.

"It just doesn't make sense," she said quietly.

Pinch raised his eyebrows. "I'm sorry, dear. It's really no longer any of our business. We must leave it to the detectives." The eyebrows twitched.

"It's just. It's only, Mr Macaulay's words which you relayed to the Superintendent don't seem to make any sense."

Yes, indeed, it was none of her business, but Pinch wanted to scotch any doubts before they took hold. "It's really nothing to worry about, Peggy. It's an officer's job, when he's first at a place of murder, to offer some certainty for the detectives. They will uncover better evidence as their enquiries deepen and it's unlikely they'll resort to my notes. But the words are there if they need them."

"So he didn't actually say them?"

"If he didn't, they were certainly in his head. And if we had more witnesses at the scene, they would say much the same. I'm filling in the gaps, my love. Drawing a line between two known points. You mustn't worry about it."

"You're sure he killed Cedar?" she asked.

He husband sighed. "No doubt at all, and I'm sure he'll confess when he sees clearly what he's up against. He won't be able to stick to his story that he was in bed when Cedar was killed. He can have no witnesses, you understand?"

And that's how I must leave it, thought Peggy; he has no witness. She searched for some other way of showing that he could not have done it. She had already identified two awkward facts, but neither seemed to help Mr Macaulay. No one could account for Edie Snag of Bulpit Cottage for an hour each side of the crime; she didn't come hurrying when the body was found. And, although Doctor Dawes promised to collect the retired schoolmistress at four o'clock, he returned to the village in the meantime; he was seen up and down The Street.

"You must let me know if I can help."

"No, Mrs Pinch. You are to play no part in this. No part whatsoever." He looked through the window for a moment, then said, "But it may be that you can settle one matter for me. Mollie Sweatman has said something."

Peggy steeled herself not to look up from her needlework. She wanted to hold her breath. She wanted to make her ears buzz so that she couldn't hear what he was going to say.

"Remember, I went for a walk last night. I was after some of Meggastones' liquid manure. I don't doubt you guessed as much."

"You are playful rivals," said Peggy.

"I overheard Mollie and Macaulay in the churchyard. They were talking nonsense, of course, but she spoke of you."

"Me, Pinch?"

"She called you Peggy of the Wishing Pool."

Peggy pouted and shook her head. "I can't imagine why."

"Something from long ago, I should think. I know that you were a scallywag in school."

Peggy pressed her needlework to her lap and sighed, irritably, "I was nothing of the sort. I was well behaved but, yes, when the taunts and teasing got the better of me, I would overstep the mark. Why! I am thirty years old! Why! Why must everyone judge me for things I did as a child?"

Husband and wife went quiet. They were both thinking that neighbours would see her that way until she had a child of her own, but they both knew it was a conversation to avoid.

Peggy tried to relax her voice. "I suppose," she began. "All I can think of is the evening when I caught her ... I mean, came across her ... swimming in the Wishing Pool. When I refused to join her, Mollie said some pretty dreadful things. She does, Pinch. You know she does. She can be very coarse."

Pinch got to his feet. "Three evening perambulations in every fortnight, says my Town Sergeant. In writing too, constituting an order." He stepped through to the little hall, at the bottom of the staircase, and collected his helmet from the banister post. "I think tonight is sufficiently mild to merit as one of those three opportunities."

"You're convinced he's guilty?" she persisted.

"Do you know that he's not?"

Peggy focussed on some difficult stitching so that she wouldn't need to look at him as he readied himself for his patrol and stepped out of the front door. Their marriage had never been an easy one. The difference in their ages had proved more of a hurdle than she had expected. One the eve of her wedding, marrying a man twenty six years older had seemed a common sense thing to do. Now, Peggy and Pinch seemed more distant than ever. He wasn't a clever policeman. Certainly, he wasn't a detective, but she knew that her husband was a conscientious village Constable who would get to the bottom of every rumour until he understood all that had happened that afternoon. When she stood at the window and watched him commence his walk, Peggy dabbed at her tears with a handkerchief. Macaulay had been fast asleep when the murder was done; Peggy was the only one who knew it yet she dared tell no one.

PART TWO

CHAPTER FOUR

The Old Newspaper Man

The Old Man liked to say that the Cheriton was a pimple on the backside of Fleet Street; he spent much of each day playing the irritant in the pubs of the newspapermen. He had worked hereabouts since the days when he had been a school truant and, although few people on the street knew, exactly, where he worked, he had developed an image of himself that was essential to any picture of Fleet Street life. He knew that more than one artist had published sketches that showed him standing at a bar's end or, more famously, on the corner of the thoroughfare when the two o'clock watercart commenced its work. Once, he had been drawn looking up at Fetter's statue of John Wilkes; his inclusion had started by accident but the Old Man, knowing that this would be the most important picture of him, had posed carefully with his hands in his trouser pockets and his jacket tails tucked behind him. He had not seen the finished work but he regularly browsed Farringdon Street and Charing Cross Road, hoping one day to come across a broken old book with the picture in it. When he wasn't in the pubs or on the pavements, he spent his time chatting in the plush tobacco shops; the Old Man argued that the world knew no better talkers than the pipe and tobacco sellers.

The Cheriton was a Christian newsletter produced in two wooden offices, ninety-seven paces from a Fleet Street pavement. He insisted that everyone on the firm should call these ramshackle rooms the Pavilion. The establishment looked as if it had been stolen from a village green and placed on the flat roof of a smoke-blackened building which, in turn, looked as if it should have been built somewhere else. The Cheriton's office did not even merit an address; anyone wishing to correspond wrote to the editor, care of the tailor's shop two floors below.

"Pepys!"

'The Firm' was the Old Man and two others. Mrs Duffle was in charge of typing, provisions, the post and cleaning. Although she rarely knew where the Old Man was, she managed to give the impression that he was only ever a few minutes away. Sometimes, she didn't see him for days but she knew that he would appear at the Pavilion late on Wednesday evenings and work through the night until he had written every word of the next number. But today was odd. Today was Tuesday, not even tea time, and the Old Man was at his desk.

"I said, Pepys!"

Henry Peters was the other member of this modest team. He was fourteen years old and lived alone with his mother in half the downstairs of a house in Ampton Street. Henry wanted to be a newspaper reporter one day but both the Old Man and 'Duffles' were strict that he was employed to run errands and wasn't to touch other matters. He spent most of his time with the tailor downstairs.

"Pepys!"

Downstairs, Henry jumped from the tailor's chair and, with his Woodbine held high in the air, looked around for somewhere to put the cigarette. The tailor collected it from the boy's fingers as he rushed from the room. The editor shouted for a fourth time and Peters shouted back. He was bounding up the staircase, two steps at a time, carefully avoiding those patches of wood that he knew to be rotten, and grabbing the handrail only when he knew it was safe. At the turn of the second landing, the banister knob fell to the floor. He dithered. He decided to put it right on his return, rushed halfway up the next flight, then changed his mind and came back to screw the knob back into place.

"Where is that boy!"

Mrs Duffle continued typing, expecting the youth to arrive at any moment, clutching his cloth cap in one hand while the other screwed up a coloured handkerchief inside his pocket. She typed in an erect position because, although a shoelace was looped around her spectacles, they fell off if she nodded.

"He's shouting for me," Peters panted as he fell through the door.

"Where's your cap?" she asked.

"Downstairs," he said.

She blinked deliberately, indicating without a further word that he should go straight into the Old Man's office. She always pretended that, concerning Pepys, she and the Old Man worked in concert, which meant that Henry was on the outside and Duffles was one up on him. Pepys thought she had a dog's face. He said that she had skin the colour of mustard and, since she had blackheads on her cheeks, it was coarse mustard.

"Mr Hardcastle, sir?"

"Yes sir. Master Pepys, sir. It's all twaddle." Sixteen years ago, the Old Man had bought a secondhand chair, constructed for a very large man. He had placed it behind his desk and declared an ambition to fill the space. Now, he could lean back in the chair and read with a book balanced on his belly. He worked with his braces down and, although he was generally careful to lever them back into place before moving, his party trick was to wedge himself so that he could stand and take the chair with him. His voice had the depth and breadth of a roar. It seemed to come up from the dungeon, as if his body provided one giant set of bellows. He liked to think that he was playful in what he said but he knew, if he caught the wrong tone, he could frighten the boy.

Henry spluttered, "Twaddle, sir. Yes sir. What is?"

"You weren't sick last week. Your mother says she saw neither hide nor hair of you. What's more, you weren't with your Uncle Smith. Up to no good, Pepys!

"Sir, I was properly sick, I promise."

"I have a job for you."

"A job for me, Mr Hardcastle," Henry repeated, yet to venture further than the office door.

"Yes, Pepys. A long job."

41

Henry blinked. A job as far as Aldersgate, he hoped, so that he could catch a bus home without returning to the Pavilion.

"I want you to go to a village, halfway between Waterloo and Southampton and lodge at the inn for ten days."

"Waterloo and Southampton," Henry confirmed, and nodded. He was still blinking. He wanted 'Duffles' to join him at the door so that she could check the details with him when the Old Man had finished. But the typing didn't falter. Clicker-clicker it went and, after every three bars, a bell tinged. Oh please, Duffles, he thought; you know I get things wrong.

"You will catch the four-fifty."

"Ten days, Mr Hardcastle," said Henry, understanding none of it.

"People are murderin' each other, Pepys."

"Yes, sir. Murdering."

"In the quiet and peaceful villages of England. Parish souls in turmoil, wouldn't you say? A congregation adrift and looking for penitence. I want you to stay in the Red Lion for two weeks and come back with a story."

"A story, Mr Hardcastle? You want Pepys to write a column?"

The Old Man inclined his head. (He would not indulge the lad with a smile.) "Keep in touch. A telephone call to Duffle each day. And Pepys, you are seventeen."

"No, Mr Hardcastle. Fourteen." The lad always placed 'a' after 'r', saying four-a-teen so that he sounded like a sailor, the editor thought.

"Yes, Mr Hardcastle," mocked the Old Man. "Seventeen, Mr Hardcastle. Pepys, I know the fine landlady of the Red Lion and she'll not have a fourteen year old staying with her, though God knows why. So I've told her you're seventeen and she says she's very happy to keep an eye on you."

"Keep an eye on me. Yes, Mr Hardcastle."

The Old Man watched the youth's face cloud with practicalities.

"The four-fifty, Mr Hardcastle. I'll have to leave now so Mother can pack a bag."

"I have already spoken to the unfortunate Mrs Pepys. How else did I learn of your truancy? A kitbag is on its way and should arrive at our fine tailor's door before many more minutes."

"Mother is coming here?" asked Henry. She had never been near the office before, as far as he knew.

"No, no. Busmen, postmen, candlestick makers and haberdashers. Urchins and ne'er do wells. Holy men and worthy veterans. All ready to play their part as the Cheriton Irregulars. Pepys, the whole of London town is at your employer's bidding. Never doubt it. To convey a solitary kitbag from one end of the river to the other is hardly a problem. Be gone, Pepys. Be gone"

"Sir!"

"And Pepys ..."

"Sir?"

"... You are Pepys. Pepys, you are Pepys. Neither offer nor answer any other name."

The Old Man returned to his almanac and Henry turned his back, almost ready to run, but another thought turned him round in a circle.

"Mr Hardcastle?"

"Pepys?"

"I don't understand. Why?"

"Just that," the Old Man said without lifting his head. "No one understands why. I want you to come back and tell us why."

Duffle smiled thinly as Pepys turned on his heels and scuttled away, so excited that he was broadcasting news of his mission before the tailor had any chance of hearing. The kitbag arrived, the tailor pressed a tanner into his hand – "For something on the train, young Henry" – and the fledgling stumbled uncertainly from the nest.

For an hour and a half, Hardcastle and Duffle worked at their desks without disturbing each other, though the door between them was open. Duffle made up the petty cash ledger while Hardcastle wrote a letter. It was addressed to the Old School Cottage and began with 'My dear Clemmie.' Hardcastle wrote fluently because letters to the schoolma'am were easy to write. When, at the end of their day, Duffle offered to post the letter with the rest of the office bundle, her employer hesitated. Then he calculated that giving Duffle the errand would grant him more time in the alehouse.

With time to spare, Pepys hurried through that part of London where every street name harks back to yet another trade. He skipped off and on the pavement as he entered a gently bending road and read the name of a dead man, as his mother had told him, above each shop front. 'Not a live one amongst them and should a man ever try to break the rule, he'll be dead within thirty nights.'

Without slowing down, he crossed the river and ran into the rugged, delicious smoke of Waterloo Station. Like the smell of secondhand shag, spilt beer and spitted-out chewing liquorice, the smell of working trains was a smell that made men of boys. He took strong coffee in the refreshment room, knowing that he was on a far more exciting mission than the tea and weak cordial drinkers. He hesitated at the platform gate, marking the moment when his adventure began for real. And when he was leaning forward in his seat and watching the lives of others roll by beyond the window as, in his head, he made fun of other passengers, Pepys caught the romance of undeserved travel. He kept his hand pressed in his trousers' left pocket, clutching more money than a full week's wages. Two pounds notes, a ten shilling note, two half crowns, a bob and loose coppers. And he had a return ticket and a room already booked at the local inn, where more money would be credited if he needed it. This start to his journey was very different from his last visit to the village, when he had avoided people by day and slept in the open at night.

As the train rattled and jolted its way through London's hinterland, Pepys sunk into memories of the tales of Nelson Lee, Nick Carter, Sexton Blake, Dixon and a score of others. For the next ten days he would be an adventurer, just like those heroes. Yes, he would be Pepys, the Boy Detective. 'Pepys, you are Pepys!' He wanted the fat woman, seated opposite, to ask where he was going and what he was up to. He wanted a ticket inspector to appear, to eye him suspiciously and to enquire as to his business. "Investigatin'" Pepys would say and know that, for once, he would be justified in denying further explanation to a grown-up.

CHAPTER FIVE

A Poor Church Mouse ...

Edie Snag gripped the straps of her handbag and stuttered, "I think we should do something." She nodded. "We should take measures."

Postmistress Mary, grey before her time, kept her head down as she scratched away at a pocket ledger that was nothing to do with Post Office business. Because Mrs Becker had just left the shop, she and Martha Hornsby thought that their puppy-like friend was worried about the bruises on that woman's face.

"You know I won't interfere," sprouted Mrs Hornsby. "I don't know why people expect me to be the one." The others didn't comment, so she explained, "The one to interfere, I mean." Then: "What happens indoors stays there, and who's to say it's not her just deserts?"

The Postmistress was totting up, keeping totals on her outstretched fingers, the tips of her lips and blinks of her eyelids. The other two women didn't know what the figures were about. Birthdays, Edie thought; when a woman wants to keep figures to herself, it's often birthdays. But Mrs Hornsby was sure that the Postmistess was doing something wrong. Couldn't be betting, could it? Surely, she's not counting betting slips?

The bell rang as Peggy Pinch stepped into the shop. Mrs Hornsby cocked her nose in the air and nudged Edie to do the same. 'Here's the one,' she mouthed silently. 'Above herself,' she nodded. She dared to whisper, "Knows more than she says about certain things, I'll be bound."

Grateful that she needn't be part of any conversation, Peggy stayed at the back and pretended to study the carved advertisement for boot blacking. She didn't need any. Mr Pinch acquired the household's polish from the Police Station in town. She always thought the Post Office smelt of old string and tasted of husky toffee, and everything had the colours of different vinegars. During her childhood, before Mary took over, Peggy visited this shop every day and gazed at the shelves of wood and rope toys. She remembered her jealousy when Betty Drop secured a blue and silver clown. Peggy had plotted against the girl in the schoolroom for months. When Betty died of flu, in the year that Peggy's father died, Peggy searched the empty cottage, only to learn that the clown had been passed to a nephew, Lymington way. The toy was lost for good.

The voices that Peggy heard now at the counter could have been voices from long ago. There was no more wicked place for gossip than this shop before lunchtime.

"I wasn't talking about the Becker wife," Edie was explaining. "Though I do remember what my grandmother said about such-like."

Mrs Hornsby put two elbows on the counter, trying to see what the Postmistress was writing. "You don't remember anything your Grandma said, Edie. You weren't walking when she was called to account for her sins, so don't come that."

"You know what my mother told me, do you?" Edie said crossly. "You were there, were you? Listening as she said it, were you?"

"What is it we have to do something about, Edie?" the Postmistress asked mildly, hoping to stall any further argument. She flicked the notebook shut and tucked it under the official counter blotter.

"My Grandma said it was bound to happen like that. She said, once they made it against the law for a man to beat his wife, they'd do it worse without the law."

Hornsby scoffed. "She knew all about men, did she, and what's in their heads? Your Grandmamma?"

"Was only in her lifetime, they changed the rules," Edie argued reasonably.

Again, the Postmistress interrupted. "What were you saying we should put right, Edie?"

"That Ellen Mullens letting a young lad stay on his own in the Red Lion. Why, he's no more than fourteen."

"He says he's seventeen," said the Postmistress.

But Edie insisted. "No more than fourteen. Probably a runaway and his mother's fretting while we stand here. We should be telling that Ellen Mullens what's what."

Martha Hornsby said, "There wasn't a farthing in the room, Alice said, when she cleaned. What's a man doing, away from home and not a penny on him?" To lend credence to her speculation, she tutted, nodded and pursed her lips.

Martha Hornsby had been one of the frightening grown-ups of Peggy's childhood. She had a lean, dirty looking face, disfigured by scars of old spots. Her eyes were as hard as a crow's and looked over spectacles that never sat evenly on her pointed nose. A child's mind had only to work a little to see this woman as a witch. And Martha Hornsby helped the fantasy by dressing with gothic touches and telling-off with phrases of potions and spells from Shakespeare. Peggy used to think that the woman had singled her out. "In the wrong place again, Peggity Miller!" "You can't hide things in your head, no matter how much you sulk." Peggy couldn't count the nights when she had laid awake at night, listening for every footstep on the road outside, every rattle of a gate latch, every time someone pushed against a hedge in the dark. Every tweet and squeal convinced her that Hornsby the Witch was coming for her.

Over the years, the talk had mellowed and although the Willowby and Becker children whispered that there was witchcraft in the Hornsby cottage, they didn't believe it in the way that Peggy's generation had done. Martha Hornsby had greedily garnered a reputation as the know-it-all of wicked doings in the night-time and, with her husband's help, she had carefully shifted the focus to the Professor's Lodge. Several old wives believed that eccentric spirits enticed unidentifiable virgins into that peculiar home and they were never seen again. Martha Hornsby was a malicious woman.

When Peggy looked towards the Post Office counter, she noticed how the back of this woman's neck craned forward from her coat collar and she wondered if she could get that rascal, Freddie Becker, to drop a dead mouse inside. (Peggy would have liked to share the idea with his sister but Peggy had adopted a hidden mission to discourage the girl's naughtiness.) Of course, it would be so much more fun for Peggy to play the prank herself. Then, before she could bring her imagination to heel, she was weighing the chances of getting away with it and, suddenly, these thoughts of a dead mouse had filled her head with images of Macaulay in bed. There it was, a dead mouse resting between his thighs.

"Are you all right, dear?"

Peggy realised that she had already pushed her way to the front and asked for a small card of pearl buttons.

"That's just three ha'pence, Mrs Pinch," The Postmistress wrapped them and pushed the package across the counter. "And Mollie says you've promised to settle her tally."

Peggy caught her breath. She tried to hide her surprise but she felt her face tingle. "Oh, yes. Yes, I did."

"Three and five altogether, then."

"I'm not sure," Peggy mumbled, searching her little purse. "I can't have come out with … oh, yes. I think, yes. I think I've got it." She placed shillings and sixpences, threepenny bits and penny pieces on the counter and the Postmistress counted them into her palm.

All eyes were on the coins. Edie was nodding. Hornsby chewed her lips. Peggy felt herself shrink.

"Yes, well. Well, thank you. Yes, good morning."

"Something's very odd, mark my words," Hornsby was saying as Peggy stepped backwards into The Street.

Not looking where she was going, she made young Pepys stumble over the bicycle which Edie Snag had propped beneath the hole in the wall.

"Doesn't matter, Miss." Pepys was trying to gather the sweet papers and envelopes which had fallen to the pavement.

Still red-faced and bleary-eyed, Peggy picked up an envelope, glanced at the address and handed it to him.

He wouldn't look at her. "My fault, I'm sorry." He slid the letters into the post box and hurried off.

Peggy hadn't spoken a word.

She walked up the village street, unable to lift her head. She knew that, before long, she would have to tell her husband that she had been in Macaulay's bedroom when the murder was committed, and when he called for reasons, her face would be buried in a string of 'Don't know,' 'Can't explain,' and 'I'm so ashamed.' She knew that this darkening cloud was growing heavier with each hour. Now, she had made matters worse; 3s 3½d wasn't much of a blackmail but, by paying up, Peggy had ensured that further demands would follow. Worse, she had rewarded Mollie's wickedness.

It was half past ten and should have been a good village morning. John Terras was working on the church roof; the sound of his tapping and hammering rattled down The Street. Gus Becker was mending his bicycle on a grass verge, the well-behaved Willowby children were playing on the banks of the brook, and housewives – in twos and threes – paused for a courteous word at the roadside. They watched as Peggy walked across the road. Determined not to turn her head, she tidied the contents of her small wicker basket.

If the village learned the whole story, people wouldn't only slander her or grumble about her, they would despise her; they wouldn't punish her, but they would blame her. She had seen it happen to others. Her guilt would be beyond question; they would give her no chance to recover her standing and no excuse to complain about their judgement. They would make her a scapegoat, promoting a sense that her bad behaviour was the root of the murder in their midst. For years to come, they would say that anything base was 'like that Peggy Pinch.' All because of the sinful thing that she had done in Old School Cottage. Walking into a man's bedroom – not even a friend – when he was naked and uncovered on his bed. How could she feel hard-done-by? She had lapsed in her loyalty to her husband and her own promises to God. Peggy knew that she was despicable.

Before she was properly into her stride, she heard the patter of little feet coming up from behind. Edie Snag in a hurry always gave an odd impression that nothing was moving above her knees because her shoes were too big and she had to trot in quick tiny steps. She wore a cheap beret pinned to the top of her head, a fur jacket which had belonged to someone much posher, and a wide flowing skirt (out of fashion) with a ragged hem where Edie had stitched it. She held her handbag before her, her fingers gripping it and fidgeting. "You're going to Church," she said excitedly, hoping that Peggy would let her catch up. "Why are you going to Church?"

"Hello, Edie."

"Are you going to speak with Miss Carstairs? She's bound to be there, it being today. She's always there on this day, thinking over the mite's grave. Is that why you're going?"

"Where's your bicycle, Edie?"

"I can go back for it," she replied simply. "What will you be doing in Church?"

"I want to pray, Edie, that's all."

"Will you see the Vicar? You will talk to him for me, won't you? It's unfair, him wanting to close my library."

"Don't worry, Edie. No one is going to touch the library. It belongs to us all."

"Miss Carstairs was saying we should put another penny a week on the subscription, but we don't need to, Peggy."

"When did she say that, Edie?"

"And she said she's already had a word with the Vicar and he won't change his mind."

Peggy wanted to quicken her pace but she would have been harsh to lose the little woman; Edie Snag meant no harm. "Don't worry, I said."

"We were in the library together on the morning of the awful murder. Miss Carstairs said it all needed seeing to. Peggy, I think it's wrong what the Vicar did, stopping Mr Meggastones from the ringing the alarm when your Arthur said he should. But, the Vicar is the Vicar, you do see that?"

"When Pinch explained that we always ring the bell, the Vicar said go ahead. He didn't understand, Edie"

"But they're not talking, are they?" She shook her woolly head. "It's not right, not right at all. Is Mollie Sweatman blackmailing you?"

"What a wicked thing to say. Of course, she's not."

"I think she is. That's why you settled her tab."

Peggy felt that everyone was paying attention, not only the folk in The Street but people in their homes, dusting shelves, knitting in armchairs or baking with a door open. She pictured a face at every window and ears pressed to every cranny. Someone was working shears behind a hedge; the noise stopped and Peggy imagined the gardener leaning forward to catch every word.

"What does she know about you, Peg?" Edie asked, concerned for her neighbour.

"Nothing, Edie. Why, whatever makes you think that she's threatening me? You mustn't spread such nonsense."

"Will you carry on paying? You'll have to, I suppose."

Peggy stopped at the top of The Street and allowed Edie to draw close to her. "I can't have you talking like this, Edie, not even when we are alone. I'm your friend, and you are mine, aren't you? Then you must not give people hereabouts reason to tittle-tattle, and our talking in huddles does just that. Now, run along and collect your bike before Freddie Becker makes of with it and teases you."

Peggy's tone made the little lady feel special. She was sure that the policeman's wife spoke to no one else like this. She glowed – not with embarrassment, not with pride, but with the warmth of a child who has been put to bed with a kiss. She stepped back without looking where she was treading, tied her fingers in knots and pulled a funny face as she tried to think of something to say.

"I'll see you tomorrow, Edie, after the service. Stay indoors and keep it warm and I'll come round for tea."

"Oh yes. I always light the fire before Church so it will be really cosy." She hurried away. She was halfway to Bulpit Cottage when she turned and shouted, "We'll be able to count the books in the library!"

Peggy watched and decided that little Edie Snag was probably the best loved person in the village, yet no one would think of saying so. Martha Hornsby had got no further than the Post Office step and, although Edie all-but bumped into her, the witch-woman seemed not to notice her. Mrs Becker, kneeling at her hedge as she trimmed it, heard Edie's squealy nonsense as the rattled the latch of Bulpit Cottage but she knew that nothing could be the matter so didn't lift her head. Edie Snag's meanderings wasted time, just like the nonsense that came out of the wireless.

When Peggy walked through the kissing gate at the side of the churchyard, Miss Carstairs was tidying the tiny grave of one of her schoolchildren who had died on the day of the King's Coronation, sixteen years before. The father was killed in the War and the mother no longer came to the village, so Miss Carstairs had quietly adopted the grave. John Terras was using the dry day to clear the drudge from the church battlements. He had a reputation for slow thorough work and it made no difference that this job was without pay. She knew that John's horse would be standing on the blind side of the church, content in her shafts. St Stephens stood at a crest with the village falling away on one side and a patchwork valley of woods and farmland on the other. As Peggy reached the brow, she picked up the sounds from the saw mill far away. She walked along the down trodden path that separated the rich graves from the poor graves and watched for Miss Carstairs looking over her shoulder or John looking down from the top, but Peggy got to the church without being noticed. She delayed in the porch, touching the notices – some typed but many handwritten – tacked to the timber struts of the little shelter, and listening for a clue that anyone else was inside. Delaying the reckoning would not make it easier so she pushed against the heavy door. She was relieved to see that Ruby Becker had already freshened up the flowers and she remembered that one of the few good things about the new Vicar was that he didn't creep about the church as his predecessor had done. But the quiet and emptiness brought no peace. Peggy was immediately aware of the familiar inscriptions on the walls, the fresco and carvings, the pews where she had sat as a child, the step where she had knelt for her first communion; today these things weren't comforts but stern judges that rose up at her, demanding recompense.

Peggy sat in the second row of pews. She bowed her head but she couldn't forbid the demons that pressed her. Unable to resist, she turned her head and imagined, high up, an image of Macaulay hanging. His neck was broken at a hideous angle, his toes and knees turned inwards and his elbows seemed pinned behind him in an unnatural form. The vision was with her for only an instant, yet it was vivid and animated and when it was gone, its taste stayed in her mouth. Still unable to cry, she leaned forward. This time, when she opened her eyes, she saw the man on his bed, his legs twisted and stretching so that, if she held onto the picture, she would see him again, exposed.

She didn't need these intrusions. She already knew that too much was her own fault, that Macaulay would be executed because Peggy Pinch would be unable to admit that she had crept into his bedroom and watched him asleep. Discovering the identity of the murderer would not put things right but failing to find out the truth would make matters so much worse. She had come here to pray but she found that she couldn't ask for forgiveness or understanding. Neither could she let things be. Duty? It was something very close to that.

She couldn't bring words together in a prayer but she summoned every sinew of her faith. But she was horribly conscious that her bad ways had made a fraud of her beliefs. She lifted her head and beseeched the stained glass window at the head of the church. Surely, there must be a way through this. She found herself calling on the strength of her mother's faith. She felt ashamed, she felt disobedient and full of shortcomings. More than anything she felt gluttonous and dirty. How could she say that she hadn't been greedy for sin when she walked into the bare man's bedroom?

Her mother, widowed by the big flu and poor to the end of her life, had known how to deal with a daughter who went too far. 'Blame yourself' she had called sternly, one night when Peggy was weeping halfway up the stairs after a good telling off, 'but don't make a virtue of it.' Little Peg had been too young to understand the ins and outs of the dictum but she understood that she should cry real tears and, once cried, she should be done with them. Now, Peggy was talking to her God as a child might do. She would be good, she wanted to say. She promised she would.

She stepped out of the pew and, turning round, saw that Queen O' Scots had crept into the church and, having delivered something at her feet, was seated patiently, waiting for Peggy's response. At once, Peggy was able to read the quizzical expression on the cat's face. This time, Queen O'Scots wasn't sure she had done the right thing. Peggy stooped and found the dead little mouse on the ground, between the cat's legs. "Well, now. Good morning, Mr Capability Mouse."

CHAPTER SIX

... And His Capabilities

"Why, Queenie," Peggy smiled. "Sometimes I think that no one knows me better. Nothing passes through my head without your sensing it." She collected the corpse by its tail, wrapped it in a handkerchief and dropped it into her handbag. She fondled the cat's shoulders and neck, and when Queenie responded, pressing herself against Peggy's legs, she said "Can you and I really be thinking of such a prank, Queenie, in our church?"

Then a shadow passed through the light from a window and Peggy stood back. "Vicar!"

The cat was gone. The handbag was hidden behind Peggy's back. She wobbled her shoe pretending that something was hurting.

"Such lovely flowers," he said. "Mrs Becker does a grand job, don't you think. I was wondering if it's all too much for her and we might draw up a rota. What do you think?"

"I don't think that at all!" said Peggy. They looked at each other for a few awkward moments, both surprised by the sharpness in her voice. "I mean, Ruby Becker has tried for so long to find something she's good at. She feels that, well, she owes rather a lot to the village, after her Dorothy's illness, and the flowers are her way of putting something back. It would upset her if she thought any one of us wasn't satisfied with her efforts. Really, you'd do well to leave alone, Reverend."

"I was thinking aloud. Wondering, that's all." He marched towards her and Peggy had an uncomfortable feeling that he was going to offer to shake her hand. Everyone said he had so little idea of manners in their proper place. "Mrs Pinch, I was told that the parish would be uncertain, confused, and even suspicious because my predecessor had left in ..." He was hesitating again.

"Under a cloud," Peggy nodded.

"It's going to take me longer than I had hoped to build trust and confidence."

"Well," said Peggy, meaning business. After all, she might as well say it, now he was listening. "You won't help matters by threatening to take over the lending library. You have no idea how hard we have all worked and Edie is so proud of it."

"No, no. I didn't mean to ... oh, dear. I had better put things right. I must see Edie this morning."

"No. You'd do better speaking with Miss Carstairs so that she can patch matters neatly. We'd want to avoid any awkwardness, wouldn't we?"

He was stepping forward again. "Mrs Pinch, there is one matter in which I desperately need your assistance. PC Pinch and myself seem to rub each other the wrong way, and I must see him urgently. I mean, well, later on this afternoon perhaps. Do you think you could have a few words with him beforehand? To smooth the path, so to speak."

"He lunches early. He'll be finished by half past twelve and likes to nap until ten-to. Would that be sufficient? Ten minutes at ten to one."

Peggy didn't want to be any more helpful. She was already walking out of the church. What was it about that man that made her feel so crotchety? She left him standing there.

'He always wants to come too close,' she reflected as she trod across the grass of the graveyard. 'And his eyes; they do too much looking.'

"Manners. His manners are too bad for a Vicar."

Miss Carstairs was standing at the post and rail fence, looking across the farms and woodlands. Peggy was muttering aloud as she approached her from behind. "I mean all clergymen are odd. Because they aren't normal. Not in the normal world. Don't really understand people. But this one gets too close. Even closer than you'd expect." Then, loud enough to make the old schoolmistress turn around: "Ah, Miss Carstairs!"

"Oh Peggy dear." She might have been saying, 'calm down' or

'whatever it is, doesn't matter so much.' "You were muttering. You're no better now than the days when you were Peggity Miller. I told you then, didn't I? You've no talent for composition. Speak as your nature says and let those who will be clever."

Peggy smiled at the classroom rebuke. "Edie reminded me that you'd want to be with Minerva this morning," she said.

"Just for a few minutes. It's her twenty-first, but I don't need to make too much of it."

Peggy knew that the schoolmistress tended the grave each week and that this morning's visit was an opportunity for a simple prayer, that's all. "It's a lovely valley, isn't it?" she said, collecting her thoughts. "We're very lucky."

The old schoolmistress drew in deeply. "Her kindergarten is a good idea," she said. "I can't say that it's not and, really, her accent is no problem at all."

Peggy stayed a step behind. "The children of the village still love you, Miss Carstairs."

"But she is so regimented. Everything in twos and one behind the other, and she makes them learn by repeating together. I've tried to tell her that country children need room to spread but ..." She took another deep breath. "Of course, she's right not to listen. Yes, Peggy, such lovely countryside."

The boundary fence provided the best view of the farmlands beyond the village. The little community had clubs for birdwatchers, botanists, would-be archaeologists and artists and, when the Wishing Pool was too far and the village ford too messy, the hobbyists would bring their field glasses and sketchpads to this fence. There had been talk of a troop of lady dancers from town who wanted to 'discover themselves' in the churchyard at night but when the Verger received a deputation of wives and mothers, he promised that nothing would come of the idea. 'Rules Against Camping' was the latest campaign of the Post Office women. The village accepted the knights of the road, the gypsies and travelling showmen who passed their way every year or two, but folk objected to suburbanists with their phoney notions of fresh air and country teachings. 'If they want to get close to the land,' said Jones of Thurrock's Farm, 'they should give up their warm town houses and work our soil.'

About three quarters of a mile away, half a dozen gentlemen – in sports gear but with no guns or dogs – were grouped around two motorcars, parked off a farm track. They were talking and pointing, considering and disputing. Perhaps because the women were looking downhill, or because the men were standing at odds to the sunlight, they all looked as if they were wearing hats that were too large.

"I want to know what those city types are about," said Miss Carstairs. "Too smart to be trippers, and look at the way they are discussing matters. They're working at something, Peggy. Surveyors, I'd say. Or businessmen with ideas."

"Well, they won't be newspaper men, will they? You've made sure of that. I think your friend, Mr S.C. Hardcastle has told the big papers to stay away. They agreed that he could send young Pepys to alert them of any developments. He must be very influential, your friend, Mr Hardcastle." Peggy explained, "I saw his name before Pepys posted the envelope. I recognised it at once but couldn't put my finger on the time and place. I should have been sharper."

"You were only a schoolgirl, Peggy."

"And he was the school inspector? You were both very discreet. No one thought that you were close."

"I shall have to tell Pinch. He'll want me to swear a statement before the detectives."

"Does it bear on the murder?"

"I knew that the story would come out sooner or later, and I wanted you to be the first to know. I've always wanted you to discover the truth while it was still a secret. He never deceived me. We knew from the start that there could be no future for us while he was married. Cedar would never have given him a divorce – and why should she? She'd done nothing wrong. But when their life together grew too stormy, she promised to leave him. She would disappear, she said. She left enough clues for the world to guess that she had drowned herself off Gilkicker Point but, of course, with no body, Selwyn could not marry again. She had left him, but he would never be free."

"But surely, doesn't the law say after a year and a day, or seven years, is it?"

"Cedar became Cedric and moved into the village. She made it clear that if Selwyn and I tried to find any happiness together, she would reappear as herself. She had the last laugh."

Peggy nodded. "What a spiteful woman."

"Not at all. I had no business making friends with her husband, but she never let me see that she was angry with me. She was always polite. Do you know, I grew to like her a little? We had begun to spend an afternoon together each month. We shared something, don't you see? We both loved Selwyn but that love had brought us sadness."

Peggy was so confused by the revelation that she felt the earth's orbit had suffered a hiccup. Each of Miss Carstairs' children believed that they were special to the village schoolmistress, but that premise had been especially important to Peggy. During the difficult years, when she had grown from a girl to a woman, she was sure that Miss Carstairs was the only person who properly understood her. And although she had grown up before she lost her parents, Miss Carstairs moved gently to fill the gap. She was Peggy's mentor. Peggy had spent the evening before her marriage in Old School Cottage and Miss Carstairs had spoken so wisely that night that, four years later, Peggy couldn't believe that life had caught her out. Then, there was the physical side of the story. The schoolma'am seemed such a secure person, buttoned up and soundly shod, that Peggy couldn't imagine her allowing a man to kiss her or touch her tenderly. And any thought that she had been in bed with a man was as obscene as picturing her own parents making love.

"Miss Carstairs, you and Doctor Dawes knew the truth of her identity. Did anyone else?"

"I've said that I do wonder if Cedar had known the new Vicar's wife. She was certainly worried about her impending arrival. She spoke of a new woman in the Vicarage bringing things to a head."

"And Mollie Sweatman? Do you think Mollie Sweatman knew?"

"Don't be silly. Peggy, you really must stop hating Mollie at every turn. You're like two spoilt children on the school quad. Why can't you worry about Dorothy and Freddie Becker instead? I can't think that we've done right by them. That poor girl nearly died of diphtheria. The house was closed up and the family shut away for two weeks. Sometimes, I think that they've never been allowed back into the village, not properly. Mothers and fathers don't like their children playing with Dorothy. You've seen how Mrs Willowby has an anxious eye when she's about. And I've seen no one go in their front or back door since the fever. Have you seen them in Church? They sit on their own on the edge of the pews, down in the dark corner." Then her attention returned to the strangers in the valley. "These gentlemen are spying out the land, Mrs Pinch. Thurrocks are planning a new road. Now, what's that all about? A merger with Home Farm, do you think? Or something more to do with our good Vicar?"

Peggy said, "He wants to see Pinch urgently." But she was still thinking, 'I don't like the way he looks at people.'

Miss Carstairs was considering this new fact when the Vicar came striding across the graveyard, the tail of his sportsjacket flapping behind him, his Cambridge scarf flying free. "It can't be! Oh, they mustn't!" When he reached the two women he leaned so heavily over the top rail of the fence that the posts creaked in their footings. "No one's ready for them." He was trying to wave away the party of gentlemen but they were too far off to notice. He turned to Peggy, "Mrs Pinch, you must bring forward my meeting with your husband. I am sure it becomes an emergency."

Miss Carstairs stalled any response. "Now Vicar," she said softly, reflecting that this wasn't the first village Vicar she had calmed down and there would probably be others to come. "First, we need to set out the facts, don't you think?" She linked a comforting arm with his and led him back towards the church. Peggy smiled as she heard her suggest a cup of tea in the Vestry.

She trod towards the churchyard gate, wanting to walk slowly home and let the muddle and ripples of the village settle down while she was indoors. She thought she might do some mending. But Peggy wasn't clear of the kissing gate before she heard excited squeals from ginger-topped Freddie, the Becker's naughtiest child. The short-trousered scamp ran like a terrier across the green and into Wretched Lane, crying hysterical tears and clutching his fly buttons. The reason for his excitement was clear: Witch-woman

Hornsby was striding up The Street, stamping a gnarled stick on the ground with each step. It was more like a staff than a walking stick. The set of her pointed face and her vice-like grip on the pole made matters clear. Little Freddie had played a trick on her and, though he had scampered away and she had no chance of catching him, the woman was determined to have it out with him.

She marched twenty yards along Wretched Lane and stopped. She wasn't sure if he had ran down the Waddie to his back gate, or found a hiding place in the trees, or carried on running to the end of the lane and into the fields. She stood sentry at a gap in the hazel hedge, looking left and right, stepping forward but seeing nothing, then coming back to the hedge.

Peggy saw her chance. She could easily creep up behind the woman, sheltered by the hedge, and drop the dead mouse down the back of her coat. So easy, thought Peggy, and she took two or three steps to see if she would be detected.

From twelve doors down, Ruby Becker's exasperated plea flew across the rooftops. "What have you been doing! Freddie, I don't know what to do with you! You tell Mother the truth, do you hear!"

Martha Hornsby didn't move. Her wooden staff tapped on the stony ground as she weighed matters in her mind.

Peggy stepped quietly through the long grass of the churchyard's edge, her hand already exploring the inside of her handbag. When Mrs Hornsby's neck was less than ten feet from her, Peggy's fingers curled around the hidden handkerchief and, finding Mr Capability's tail, got ready to bring him out.

She was sure that she could get away with it. The Vicar and the schoolmistress were occupied in the Vestry. It was eleven o'clock; Pinch would be standing at the War Memorial, having spent ten minutes with his pipe behind the Red Lion. No one else was walking up The Street, and no one could warn her.

She was ready to step back if Mrs Hornsby turned around. But Mrs Hornsby didn't. Peggy counted to three in her head, then lifted the mouse to the top of her handbag.

A strident voice yelped from the trees. "What are you doing, Peggy Pinch?"

How long had Mollie Sweatman been watching? Peggy dropped the mouse back into the hiding place and jumped back so that, when Hornsby turned around she was a polite distance away.

"Mrs Hornsby, I was wondering …. " though she had no idea what she could have been wondering.

"I said, what are you doing!" shouted Mollie, rushing towards them.

"Don't you spy on me, Peggy Pinch," warned Hornsby. She said, "I know just what you're up to," and, without further challenge, marched off in the direction of the church green.

Now, Miss Carstairs was coming towards them.

"Mollie, please don't say anything."

Her enemy's face was laughing at her, new ideas and spiteful tricks in her head.

"One thing more!" The Vicar called from St Stephen's porch. "Miss Carstairs, I'll catch you up."

Peggy feared that she would soon be surrounded and Mollie would tell everyone what she had been doing when Cedar Wells was killed.

"Mollie, please."

"I want another one and six."

"Yes, yes. But, please."

"Don't think you can talk your way out of it. One and six or I tell your husband where you were when Wells was knocked down."

Peggy knew that there could be no arguing with her. She had known Mollie since their childhoods. The woman had been horrid then, she was horrid now and horrid ever would be.

"I won't be able to spare the money until Friday," she said desperately. Miss Carstairs and the Vicar were only a few steps from being in earshot.

Mollie Sweatman licked her lips, then drew her pimpled, stumpy fingers across her mouth. Like a greedy girl tasting the last of her favourite lollipop. "Friday then. Just as long as we both know."

CHAPTER SEVEN

The Pipe Smokers

Pinch went without his afternoon nap and Peggy made sure that their cold lunch was cleared away before one o'clock. When the visitor arrived, Pinch was deep in his armchair with his pipe well on and his ale half drunk. Peg brought another beaker, a sister to her husband's favourite wooden mug, and some reserves in an earthen pitcher which she stood in a cool place between the bookcase and the fire. The Vicar was settling himself in the second armchair so Peggy, realising that the men would be better left alone, found things to do in the scullery. The Vicar was complaining courteously about something he had read in the morning paper.

An open wooden pot of tobacco sat on the low table, no larger than a square meal. The Vicar brought an empty pipe from his pocket and Pinch nudged the baccy his way.

"Ah, thank you." The Vicar recognised the brand at once. "Cohen and Weenen?"

Pinch nodded.

"My father-in-law has always wanted to visit their shop in Charing Cross Road," said the Vicar as he worked with his pipe. "But that's out of the question now. A stroke has left him as good as dumb and useless down one side. My Isabelle won't be joining me until her father has a proper nurse in place."

"I'm sorry to hear that," said Pinch and there was an unspoken resolution that the matter would not be addressed further.

Pinch observed a man who liked to pack the bottom of his bowl tightly, allow a looser knot in the middle and finely rub some shreds on top, making the pipe easier to light. Not a countryman's way, Pinch reflected. Likely, the Vicar had practised smoking in the clubrooms of posh people.

"The village needs your help, Mr Pinch," he said as his match still hovered over his pipe. "We're to be bothered by troublesome weather."

Pinch nodded his head. "Edie Snag's settling."

"No, no. Something more pressing."

The policeman inclined his head but made no other reply.

Soon there came the happy communion of two men who drew on their pipes in similar depth and speed. Smoke didn't puff into the air, like it does from busy trains. Rather, it twirled and wafted like smoke from the last village chimneys at half past ten. Pinch was confident that the fug wouldn't be spoilt by blue smoke, a sign of a man who doesn't know when to let his pipe rest. A crick of Pinch's neck encouraged the Vicar to get on with his beer. Pinch's was all but drunk and he didn't want to replenish his beaker until the Vicar was ready for a top up.

The Vicar judged that it was time to take his pipe from his mouth for half a minute or so. Smoking wasn't only about drawing good flavour inwards; he knew that he should deliver no more than the right amount of smoke into the room.

"You came to speak about tomorrow morning?" suggested Pinch, reaching for the reserves of ale.

"Tomorrow? You want to speak at the service? I hope you will. I've …" The Vicar hesitated. He was on the edge of something that he had yet to settle in his own mind. "I've spoken with the incumbent of St Faith's. He's been very patient with me. We've left the question open and, at the moment, I sense that it might be welcomed if he, not I, brought the parish together in the morning. I've got off on the wrong foot with so many of you."

Begin, Pinch thought, by finding yourself. Get your bearings, young man.

Suds of textured ale clung to the sides of his beaker as if only a little encouragement would start it fermenting some more. He reached for the pitcher, poured a half pint for himself and, without asking, filled the Vicar's beaker. "Edie Snag is pressing," he said.

"Look here, Pinch. I poke my nose into things with good intentions and, before I know it, matters have got out of hand. That's what happened with my speed trials. There I go again, you see. 'Speed trials'. What I mean is 'one speed trial'. I have only ever driven in one competition but people will have you believe I'm a regular motor-sporter. It started when I watched my brother tinkering with his old Vauxhall. Then, I gave him a hand with the spanners and what-not, and agreed to drive it up a hill-climb. Suddenly, I'm seen as the motor-mad cleric, and nothing could be further from the truth. I should have … I mean, I know … the thing is, I've done nothing to put the stories straight. Well, this morning I was visited by half a dozen businessmen who want to buy-up part of Thurrocks Farm and make a motor hill-climb out of it. They came to Thurrock's farm on the trail of the Doctor's Morris."

Pinch nodded. "It was left on the farm when Thurrock's father died at Farlington races. Thurrocks had no use for it and it was pushed into one of the barns. But when Edna was widowed, she insisted that Doctor Dawes should be allowed to buy it, for whatever he could afford. Dawes had helped both the old grandpa and her husband over the years." Pinched puffed, tapped the stem against his teeth and looked at the ceiling. "We were all very pleased."

"That's the story my businessmen heard. It's a Silent Six. Only fifty were made and this one was shipped to Paris. It seems that the model had a faulty design and this Frenchie fixed it up in his own way. That makes it unique and these motorists are after it. But they also saw the winding track up from the farmyard to the back of our churchyard and seized the idea that they should develop it."

"She'd be ready to sell," Pinch remarked.

"They're having problems with Shelsey it seems," The Vicar reflected, although the comment meant nothing to Pinch. "Too muddy, and I understand it slips."

"Jones from Home Farm pretty much manages Edna's affairs these days. Your friends should talk to him."

"Oh my word, that's what I must avoid! My congregation would never trust me again. Believe me, I tried so hard to dissuade them but they had answers for all of my objections." Then he pointed his pipe stem at Pinch's modest bookshelf. "Ah! I see you have a Herbert, the Compleat Angler's friend."

Pinch reached for the slim volume above the fireplace. "It's not mine, I'm afraid. One of my predecessors decided that every police house should have a library that could be passed from tenant to tenant. I found this the other day." Pinch turned to the title page then handed it to the Vicar. "Extracts From a Country Parson."

The Vicar held the old leather-bound book between his palms and let the leaves fall open. "Yes, one of my father's enthusiasms. It's nice to see a dainty copy like this."

Pinch could feel the Vicar itching to slip it in his pocket. "Please, borrow it whenever you like."

"Oh, no, no. I think I've meddled enough with our village libraries, don't you." He rubbed a thumb down the cracked joint of the leather spine, then replaced the book carefully above the fire.

"People would be sorry to see the old Morris go." Pinch glanced at the Vicar. "They called it the Doctor's Coupe, you know. But I've hear that's really a name for a Rolls Royce."

Here were two real pipe men who could fill the room with grey smoke, unspoilt by scorching or excessive use of the match. The flavours of old tobacco would enrich the polished furniture and the homely textured fabrics, while the odour of country beer masked any dryness in the room. The Vicar was a straight-stemmed man who had yet to learn how to slouch properly with a pipe. Well, every man in his own way, thought Pinch; he wasn't one to offer advice. Thank goodness, his guest wasn't one of these young men who do all they can to keep a pipe going. Clearly the Vicar had discovered the pleasure of an idle pipe; when it went out he didn't relight it straightaway but let the bowl cool and tapped it with a fingernail, bringing the tinder to the top. Pinch judged that the new incumbent might not be wise, might not be quick witted but he was good natured.

"Then I remembered my Dean going on about an old covenant on the land." The Vicar rubbed his creased forehead. "How I wish I'd listened to him. I mean, how can I admit to him now that I was half asleep when he was instructing me on local matters? Anyway, the covenant. I'm sure if I could get hold of the document it would show that this hill-climb is a non-starter. Oh, I say! A non-starter and a hill-climb! The deed is supposed to be in the parish chest. Meggastones can remember it being there but now that it's gone he's sure our strange Professor has stolen it for his own peculiar purposes. He fancies himself as a local historian, I understand. What can you tell me about him, Pinch?"

"He's done nothing bad. But I've five bob that says he was hiding behind gravestones on the night before Cedar Wells was killed."

The Vicar raised his eyebrows. "I'm sorry?"

Pinch realised he had been indiscreet and shuffled the seat of his trousers deeper into his chair. "Not that it has anything to do with the Wells murder," he began uncertainly. "Really, it's nothing. I saw Mollie Sweatman and Macaulay frolicking beneath the church elm that night. I thought it was Cedar Wells who was keeping an eye on them, but it could just as easily have been the Professor." He jerked his pipe sideways to belittle the observation. "People say he's peculiar because he won't fit in one particular basket, but that doesn't make him bad. He's a spectator – the sort of man who writes a book in secret – but he doesn't stand back. In fact, he rather pushes himself forward. I've seen him in the Red Lion from opening time to closing time and stand with every one of us. He has a knack of joining in a conversation without actually saying anything. It's uncomfortable because, well, when he's with other folk, I get the feeling that he's doing some sort of work."

The Vicar laughed. "I have met that kind."

"I've heard it said that his house is full of arty things and that would make sense. A man who keeps his own counsel is likely to see beauty where others pass it by. But if he's got your rectory covenant, he'll treat it like a treasure. It will come to no harm."

"But how do we get it back? How do we even suggest that we suspect he has taken it? I mean, we can hardly turn up at his Lodge and demand a search. It would be different if his place was one of the church properties, but it isn't."

"Edie Snag's case is pressing, and she certainly is a church tenant."

"Miss Snag?"

"Miss Carstairs and I have been discussing. Edie's cottage is in poor repair and, though she would make an excellent housekeeper, we cannot expect her to live with unhealthy damp and growths. A move, we thought, might be in order."

"A move?"

"You need a housekeeper, Vicar, and once in the Vicarage, we're sure that she'd find a new home for the village library."

"Ah! Yes, I see."

"Of course, no one must tell her to move. Just offer her the post as your housekeeper and once she feels sure of herself, she will suggest the move, and that will be fine. The cottage can be left empty while the church estates address the repairs."

"The Bishop won't like the place being empty," the Vicar warned.

"Well, you must see that the repairs take as long as he will tolerate. Alice Tarporley and her Michael are walking out together, and everyone is sure that they'll be looking for a home before long. Why, soon after Christmas, Miss Carstairs says."

"I say. How well thought out."

"It is how we do things, Vicar."

"But what about the Professor and the missing covenant?"

"Oh, I don't think that's a problem. My Peggy will soon sort it. Leave it with me."

Pinch decided that he wouldn't patrol again that day. He knew that his report of the itinerant socialists was in the leather pouch, ready for collection when the divisional courier passed through the village. There was a bundle of recent dockets that he was required to peruse, but he left them in his bureau for another day. Unusually, he didn't change out of his uniform but slouched in his accustomed armchair, with his tie off and his collar loose and boots unlaced. He had much to digest. Pinch wasn't a sharp thinker. He pictured his mind as a muddy bog where matters arrived with a splash and wouldn't be moved but then sank beneath the thick porridge of sods and peat, to be considered later when they came up for air. Like the Doctor running up from the ford when Wells' body had been discovered; he offered no explanation of where he had been. And the stories, from so many witnesses, about the whereabouts of the Vicar's maid that couldn't be reconciled. 'She had been in all parts of the village that morning,' Pinch reflected, 'but, like a butterfly, hadn't settled in one place long enough for people to give any order to her flittering.' He pulled a copy of the Compleat Angler from its shelf, allowed it to fall open at a middle page and began to read slowly, pausing at the end of each paragraph and sometimes reading it again. (He hadn't known that Herbert had been the author's friend.)

Peg's afternoon was just as quiet. She cleaned the larder shelves and arranged them just as she liked. At three, she made herself half a pot and drank it alone in the kitchen. Then she took a small beaker of ale into Pinch, and put his slippers by the fire to warm. She took her place on the two-seater couch and read one of the paper-covered Christian novels that the Vicar's maid had passed down to her. Pinch wasn't ready to talk.

She caught herself pretending that she had no secrets to hide from her husband; it was a warm and attractive thought, but her conscience would let her hide in the daydream. As she sat there, she heard her footsteps climbing the stairs in Old School Cottage. Her face was red and she prayed that Pinch wouldn't notice. Peggy told herself, again, how lucky she was to have married a good man like Pinch, although there was much in their marriage that she hoped would change. Love takes time and sometimes it's in the nature of a man and his wife that love gets stifled and has no chance to grow. But those were matters best left to Pinch. If she conducted herself properly and worked well, he would gain more confidence in her. He would let her know when it was time to build on their lives together. Until that day, Peggy Pinch took her vows seriously; she knew where her duty rested.

He coughed, patting the breast pocket of his open tunic, then twisting his neck to see the bookshelf beside him.

Peggy rose from her seat, collected the leather tobacco pouch from the mantelpiece and passed it to the arm of his chair.

69

"Thank you, dear."

She would have liked to fill the pipe for him; after all, it could only take practice. But Pinch wouldn't want her to interfere.

When he sat forward to light the pipe, she asked, "Do you think that a husband's right to chastise a wife?"

Pinch thought, his own or another man's? He was so often amused by Mrs Pinch's loose way of talking. "Harsh words, if called for," he nodded without taking his pipe from his mouth. "Of course. How else is a woman to judge right from wrong?"

"But with his strap, Pinch, or his carpet slipper. Edie Snag was saying that her grandmother asserted that once they brought a law against it, husbands were more likely to strike out in less proper ways."

Pinch calculated vaguely: Miss Snag was born in …., so her mother was born in …, so her grandmother was born in …, so how silly of these village women to fret over what Grandma Snag might or might not have said. He often thought that wives should not be allowed to gather in groups of more than three. "You've been gossiping about the marks on Ruby Becker's face."

"Not me, Pinch. I kept well out of it." She didn't mention that she had held back because of Martha Hornsby's presence, rather than any unease about the subject.

He turned a page of his book. "I've never found it necessary," he said.

"I know. I have always said that you've never raised a hand to me. Though I fear there are few women in our parish who can say that."

He wanted to smile again. 'So, just how many women have I threaten to strike?' "You've been prattling to others about our household?"

"Only to let others know how well we are."

"Your pride is not altogether well founded," he reminded her.

"Oh, that. That was just once and hardly counts. I made you angry, Pinch. It was my fault and you didn't go as far as hitting me. I know you never will."

Their argument had been weeks ago. He hadn't said sorry at the time and he felt no need to do so now.

"So what do you think?" she persisted. "Better the thing is done in an orderly way, making it unnecessary in anger?"

"I think," said the policeman, "that if our wives and widows are given to spending time on such nonsense, it's time I stepped forward in the matter."

"Pinch?"

"The matter being the marks on Ruby Becker's cheek." He closed his book. "You were listening to my talk with the Vicar?"

"I caught one or two words as I was steaming the sheets but hardly listening, Pinch."

"We believe that the Professor has stolen an old covenant from the parish chest. A search of The Lodge should settle the question but that requires a little cleverness. I have something to put to you, Peggy. I might be asking too much."

"No, please. You must tell me." (Two days ago, he had warned her to keep away from the investigation. Now, he was asking her to take part. Just what she wanted.)

"A clandestine search is beyond us; the Professor would be too easily alerted. We must encourage him to allow a search by someone who has been invited into his home. He has always shown an interest in you, Peggy."

"He means no harm, Pinch. He's always spied on me. Really, it's no more than a silly game of peek-a-boo. It started when I was a child; he'd be waiting for me at the school gate and would follow me home. Other times, he would track me when I was running an errand for Mother. It's a joke between us. We've never spoken about it – I talk no more to that man than others do – but I'm amused when I catch his face in the bushes, or behind a hedge, or he turns up when I'm thinking of doing something that perhaps I shouldn't. He'd never hurt me."

"If you offered him the chance to play peek-a-boo as you move around his own house?"

"Oh yes, I'm sure he'd want to. Yes, he'd invite me in."

"That's the game I want you to propose. Tell him you think it's nice that he enjoys looking at you. I want you to suggest that he spies on you as you look around his place. Almost, a game of hide and seek. Then, the Vicar and I shall interrupt with a knock on the door and distract him while you delve more deeply."

Pinch had made it sound so simple, but none of the implications were lost on his wife. He wanted her to offer the Professor an opportunity to peek at her. A charade that would stimulate the Professor. Should she be pleased that her husband trusted her, or tearful that he was offering her up?

He tapped his pipe stem on the arm of his chair. "He's in the middle of this mess. I'm not saying that he murdered Cedar; I can't think of any reason why he'd want to. But he's always there. He was observing Macaulay and Mollie in the graveyard. He was on the scene in seconds when Cedar's body was found. He's never far from any development. Mark my words, if there is a second murder, the Professor will be on hand."

When the afternoon turned dull, the Professor, with his fat neck, Billy Bunter face and short sausage-like arms, sat in his study and mixed tobacco from three wooden trinkets. When he wrote, he wrote with nib and ink. He wrote by lamplight, not for any reason of his miserliness (though, Lord knows, the man was well enough known for it) but because he knew how easy it was to snoop through windows where electric bulbs burned unfettered.

Things were going well. He was pleased with the haul from his afternoon trespasses. He had spied on the three worst women in the village, collected trophies from their gardens and teased open new threads for enquiry. In the Vicarage garden, he had crouched beneath a window and eavesdropped on the new man's telephone conversation with his wife. And he had crept about the Red Lion to learn all he could about the willowy youth called Pepys. All this, and he had not once been spotted.

The Professor lived on the edge of the village. When people passed along Back Lane, the sounds were dampened by the dense shrubs and trees in his garden and his insistence of keeping all doors and windows locked. When he stayed indoors, he liked to keep everything else out. Some days he decided that he would talk to no one but himself; it was an easy thing to do.

But he was 58 and he had decided that his time was already run. He used to think that he wanted people to say that he was peculiar rather than eccentric, somebody who meant no harm but was probably better avoided. He had spent years turning his home into a warren where, should anybody be foolish enough to break in, they would be surprised by pictures that leapt forward when they turned a corner and furniture that seem to come alive because they had been placed where shadows danced. Some intruders might be disturbed by what they found (the Professor's tastes could be licentious), all would be unsettled. When the burglars left the house they would be sure that the Professor was giggling about them.

For years, he had always enjoyed the uneasiness with which others treated him. The clumsy way his neighbours kept him at arm's length. He had been amused by the nonsense of mothers drawing their children to their sides whenever he was in The Street and the conversations that dried up in mid-flow when he walked into the Post Office.

But, approaching sixty and tired of so many things, their suspicion began to irk him. Gradually, he had developed a need to get back at them. That's when he began to pinch little trinkets from them. He had chuckled to himself when, just two weeks before Cedar Wells was killed, he heard Mrs Willowby say that she was thinking of taking in laundry. Taking in laundry had been the Professor's hobby for a twelvemonth and, although he meant something that Mrs Willowby didn't, he had muttered mischievously, 'It puts you and me in the same tub,' as he followed her down the lane.

He admitted that he felt differently about his large rambling house these days. He remembered how he had poked around the attic, through one night when he had recently moved in, but decided that he wouldn't explore the trunks and haversacks that the previous occupant had left behind. He wanted The Lodge to be a house of secrets. He enjoyed not knowing what was locked away in the roof, or where the third secret passage led to, or why the stone steps in the cupboard under the staircase led not to a cellar but to nowhere at all. But he'd changed his mind. Now, he wanted to know everything about the place and had spent three weeks debating how best to map each plane. It couldn't be done as architects would do.

Mollie Sweatman was in his clutches. This delight had been neither dreamt of nor planned. Three years ago he had financed a two-penny bus ride for her. By matching his cleverness against her simplicity, he could now call on more money than her modest living could ever deliver. He didn't expect her to repay her debt. His reward was watching her fret and fidget her way through their hidden conversations. His success with poor Mollie had encouraged him to commence his Magnus Opus. *The Scurrilous Annals of an English Village*. This would be compiled as a collection of pretended correspondence with an unidentified cleric. Here, he would present his case against Mollie Sweatman; his notes were complete. His jottings about the Becker girl amounted to not very much at all, but would distress anyone who was fond of the little girl.

He had no intention that it would be published and, until now, he had admitted no thoughts that it should fuel further blackmail. No, the bound letters would be hidden in his roof so that after his death (the Professor was sure that he would expire before he was sixty) the scandals would be discovered when his estate was broken up. Although this body of his evidence against his neighbours would remain locked in a chest, upstairs, it was enough to have knowledge of other people's affairs. A man didn't need to make use of his advantages. .

But – the Professor tapped his nib menacingly on his blotting paper – he had been pressing Mollie Sweatman for so long that she had grown weary. She was becoming lax, forgetful and apt to take advantage of his patience. She needed to be taught a lesson, and the Professor had decided how to do just that.

Perhaps it was time to gain gratuities from another villager.

Peggy Pinch? No, his plans for Peggy Pinch were entirely different.

The sly Miss Carstairs? Yes, he resolved to write a first invitation before six o'clock, then he would poke his head into the inn (people were used to seeing him there and spoke without guarding their tongues) and he would be home before eight and eat well.

As, carefully and deliberately, he wrote down the truth about the old schoolma'am, the village characters moved around a chessboard in his mind, forming new alliances and changing focus. Always, there was one too many empty spaces, indicating the absence of the Vicar's wife and, always, no matter how he nudged the characters, one piece was left isolated. The parish policeman.

Before his letter was complete, the fat bespectacled misfit gave in to temptation and climbed the stairs. He was going to paw over the treasures of his afternoon's work.

His feelings for the policeman's wife had grown over these past few days. It had crept upwards like a vine, encasing him with tentacles so complicated that he couldn't fathom. For years he had looked out for her. He had looked for her as a child, as she grew up and as she succumbed to her foolish infatuation with old Arthur Pinch. The village policeman who should have known better. That's when the Professor's observations became more intrusive. He was desperate to know what went on between that husband and Peggy behind their closed doors. He longed to hear their arguments, to see her weep, to know that she regretted the pairing-off. He wanted to discover that it wasn't really a marriage at all. He had searched and stolen from the parish chest, he had travelled on long train journeys so that he could talk to people from the Constable's past. Like a scientist (after all, he was a rationalist, wasn't he?) he had written down his hypotheses of the man's fraud, then worked hard, trying to prove them.

In the middle of this work, the Macaulay man had come to the village and the Professor had noticed Peggy's immediate fascination for him. It was no more than an interest in his muscle-bound figure, the Professor told himself; she was entranced by the man's strength. So, his spying changed again; now, he was watching over her. He had often intervened anonymously, saving her from doing wrong things. But, these past two weeks, she had grown careless.

First, she had turned up at the Vicarage garden, hoping to quiz the maid about the new Vicar's wife. She hadn't noticed that Miss Mullens, returning from the parish notice board, had wandered from the church path to the garden fence so that she could eavesdrop.

The Professor hadn't been in a position to provide a distraction and, within the half hour, the Post Office women were tut-tutting about Peggy's sneaky approach to gossip. Then, the day before the murder, he had seen her pick up a toy clown at the front of the Willowby house. He had called to her this time, but she pretended not to hear and was caught by Mrs Willowby, shouting from the open front room window. Peggy promised that she wasn't taking the toy, but she offered only a lame story that she had been attracted to the clown because she had once owned a similar one.

And when Cedar Wells was murdered and the Professor had been skulking in Miss Carstairs' back garden for quite another reason, he had watched her walked blindly into Old School Cottage, drawn to the sleeping strongman by a curiosity that the Professor could not influence. She hadn't known that jealous Mollie Sweatman was watching. Peggy should have been more careful. If she was up to no good, she should have checked that she was unobserved. Really, she had no one but herself to blame if she was now in a mess.

'Did he love her?' he asked at the mirror at the top of his stairs. He pulled a noncommittal face. He believed that her presence in the village made him a better person. She was like a nutrient to his soul.

"You need to feed on her," he whispered as he knelt before the locked trunk of trophies.

CHAPTER EIGHT

Down Our Dark Alley Tonight

At midnight Dorothy and Freddie Becker were feasting on toffee biscuits that Freddie had sneaked from Mrs Hornsby's kitchen. She had been outside pegging the line, he said, but Dorothy didn't believe that. She was sure that something was going on between the witch-woman and her little brother. She blamed her for Freddie's tantrums and the desperate arguments between her parents that they boy's temper provoked. Sometimes, when she was crying and praying herself to sleep, God said that Queen O'Scots would carry the spirit of her prayers and turn Mrs Hornsby into a good woman one day. A good woman for little Freddie.

Next door, the saintly Willowby children were fast asleep. Mr had dozed off in his armchair and Mrs was taking the opportunity to polish the parlour before rousing him. Ernest Willowby was only a clerk but he worked hard. It took him an hour to cycle to work each morning; they expected him there before eight and it was usually half past six before he started for home again.

Miss Carstairs had also dropped off in her chair. She had been reading and each time she nodded the spectacles crept closer to the end of her nose. She'd be cross when she woke because she insisted that preparing well for bed was the most important habit of the day. In her dreams, she was always the active schoolmistress, never retired; she found herself back in the tiny office which she had loved for over thirty years. Sometimes, she pictured herself guiding her successor through the difficulties of running a village school, but those dreams never carried on to their end.

Edie Snag had gone to bed dead tired; she wouldn't be running outside in her carpet slippers tonight. And, although they had spent an hour drinking beer and stargazing, the Hornsbys had opted for an early night. All lights were out in their cottage. Up and down The Street, the houses were dark and there was hardly a sound in the hedgerows. The schoolma'am's cat, having moved from Pinch's shed roof to the Red Lion's waste bunkers, and from there to the soft ditch at Miss Carstairs' gate, now patrolled the top half of The Street. If she had only a morsel of luck elsewhere, she knew that the graveyard would provide a good supper. A careful listener might have heard the stilted, awkward discussion coming from the Pinches' bedroom but, that evening, there were no nosy trespassers to stand beneath the policeman's porch, as the Verger liked to do.

Seth Lovely, the Red Lion's cellarman, had finished his work and was drinking alone in the unlit bar. He rarely went to bed before half past one. It was only a few minutes past midnight, when he heard young Pepys creep down the stairs and unlatch the back door of the kitchen.

"Going for a look at the old cottage, are you, boy?" Seth whispered to himself. He brought his yachtsman's cap from the stretched pocket of his old jacket and, not forgetting his ale, followed the lad out of the pub and beyond the dray-yard. The path to the back of Bulpit Cottage was a dry ditch, taken over by soft turf. Lovely, who had come to the village as a young man, could remember the times when so much rubbish had been tipped into the ditch that it was impossible to pass. That problem had been sorted when the neighbours stayed behind, after a parish meeting, and agreed to maintain it. That was in 1915 and, through the War years, tending to the makeshift path was something that the villagers could do for the land that others were fighting for. Ten years later, Pepys could walk to Bulpit Cottage in the dark with little risk of stumbling. Seth had uneven shoulders and bow legs and walked as if he were wearing wellingtons. He didn't walk quietly, but Pepys wasn't smart enough to look behind him.

He was standing at the back gate when Seth caught up with him. "Interested in Edie Snag's little home, are you?"

"Yes. Yes, I am." Pepys rubbed his forehead. "I can't tell you why, Mr Lovely. I don't mean any mischief."

Lovely didn't want to test the youth. In the half light, he could see a lot of the lad's mother in his sallow face. The seriousness in the eyes, the sculptured shape of his nose and his habit of drawing a short breath before he spoke.

"I hope you've been looking after our skittles alley," the old man said mildly. The Red Lion had agreed to host a neighbouring team on Saturday and Pepys and Seth, always the heavy duty man, had spent the morning sanding the wooden alley and polishing the brass braces. It's more important that a village should show off the best skittles alley than win the match, Lovely had told him, although Pepys was sure that the priority would change if the Lion was losing halfway through Saturday evening. 'That's your job for tonight, lad,' old Lovely had said. 'Keep 'em off the floor while I'm not in.'

"I made sure there was no skittle playing," Pepys assured him. "What's an orlop?"

That made the cellarman laugh.

"Something on top, lad. Overlapping, see?"

"The Verger kept taunting Constable Pinch about his orlop. 'How's the orlop!' he shouted, the very moment that Mr Pinch showed his face. 'Mashing well, isn't it?' he roared. Seems to me, Constable Pinch couldn't think how to answer. Everyone laughed and banged their tankards on tabletops. I didn't know whether I should join in or not, Pinch being a Bobby. You never know with Bobbies, do you?"

But Lovely made nothing of it. "Those two are always going on about their running manure." He dug into his jacket pocket and laid a second pipe on the gatepost. "There," he said. "For you. I've been waiting for a good young 'un to pass it onto and I reckon you'll do. I've seen you with your Weights. Those city smokes will do you no good, lad, so you get used to drawing on this."

Pepys picked it up but wasn't sure what to do with it, so Lovely took it off him, packed it with a plug of Three Nuns and told him not to suck heavily when he lit it. "Draw the flame gently across the top, just whispering it in enough to get it going, but all over even like. There, like an old professional you'll be in no time."

"The Bobby was doing his rounds, all right. He as good as talked to everyone." Pepys confided, "Miss Mullens said how the Reverend's wrong not to do tomorrow's service, and Pinch reckons he'd sort it by getting a message to the other Vick over at St Faiths, telling him not to come, so our Reverend'll have to step up to the mark."

Pepys paused for breath and Seth wondered if the boy had bad lungs. Not that there'd been any lungers in the family. But then, he cautioned himself, you don't know about the other half of his make-up.

"Then Mr Pinch had a quiet word with John Terras. I caught Mr Becker's name and Terras said he'd fix it. I'm not sure but I think he's going to fix it with you. Would that be right?"

"Well, well, well," Seth laughed, man to man. "We'll make a newspaper man of you yet!"

"I've not seen the Professor since this morning, but Miss Mullens says he doesn't always come in when others are there."

"You don't have much to do with him, do you?" This time, Seth's enquiry sounded like a warning.

"He says the pictures on the walls are no good. He says they could be a lot better if someone'd give them some thought."

"Well, rightly he's justified. But you don't want to be doing much with him. He's peculiar, son."

"He'd caught me looking in the back of Bulpit Cottage, that's all. Wanted to know what I was doing. He was telling me how the lady who lived there before Miss Snag had to leave in a hurry. She was there one day and gone the next and no one asked any questions. He said as there's only one reason for a young woman to flit like that." Pepys looked down at the new pipe between his fingers. It had a short square-cut stem and a mouthpiece made from a hard shiny wood that he hadn't seen before. The bowl was shallow and had burned down on one side, and the letters RL were carved on the other. "Who gave you this, Mr Lovely? It's not yours because it's burnt down from the wrong edge."

"I may as well tell you lad, the young lady in Bulpit Cottage was mine and Gwen's daughter so the Professor's got no reason to go spreading stories. You tell him that, when next you see him."

Pepys knew that he should apologise for intruding, but he couldn't work out how to say sorry without it sounding like he wanted to know more. He stammered, "He met Mrs Pinch in the dray yard this evening. I heard them."

Seth took his time. He drew heavily on his pipe, then drained the last drop of ale from his glass. "You heard them what, lad?"

"She was inviting herself into his home. It seemed a silly thing to say, with Mr Pinch doing his rounds inside, not sixty feet away."

Twigs snapped, cotton ripped and, with a cry, Mollie Sweatman's plump body slid from a hedge not twenty yards from them. "Bloody caught myself!" she shouted. She was on her knees, straightening a dress that had twisted itself around her hips. Her white fat legs were smeared with mud and a sprig of hazel was hanging down from her bust. "Just how long are you two going to rabbit on? I've been waiting for you to go. Twenty minutes! You're like two old wives." She grabbed a rail of Edie Snag's fence and pulled herself up, first onto one knee and then, with more cursing and squawking, onto her two feet. "You want to be careful, Master What's-your-name Pepys. Saying all sorts about Peggy and the Professor. I'll tell you, you best forget all about what you saw, you young cock. You're not clever enough to gossip in this village."

Then Miss Mullens opened a window in the Lion's attic. "Get yourself abed, Mollie Sweatman! You think folk can't hear you?"

Mollie spun round, couldn't see who was shouting, so carried on spinning to a full circle. "What? Who? I never ... people round here want to ..." But she had made herself dizzy and had to reach out again.

Neither Pepys nor Seph made a move to steady her.

"What you two looking at? Not seen a girl worse for wear before? Well —-" She tested her balance. "—- Well, I'll thank you not to wonder what I've been at. Don't go pretending you haven't seen a woman's knees, Seph Lovely!"

She shook herself, straightened the dress again and wobbled her ankle until she was sure of it. Then she opened the back gate of Bulpit Cottage and walked down the side path into the village street.

Seth chewed on his pipe for a few seconds before saying, "Well, well, well. Time we were getting back, boy. There's nothing for you to learn in Edie Snag's little cotte"

He made sure they were side by side as they retraced their steps. There was a broad grin across his whiskered face. "Well, what do you think of our modest parish, lad?"

"The pub's homely," Pepys replied, avoiding any comment on Mollie's interruption. "But then, so are the London pubs and the Lion's nothing like the bars that Mr Hardcastle takes me to, or the rough houses round the streets where I live. It smells different, but the whole countryside does that, doesn't it?"

Another volley told them that Mollie had tripped over again.

"Smells, does it? How does it smell, son?"

"Like …" Pepys scratched his head. "Like stripped green wood, and the dust is more dust and less dirt. And the dirt is less dirt and more soil. You see, everything in London is because too many people are living too close. The smoke's gritty, the smells are gone-off, the way people ain't got clear tubes, it's all because people are too much on top of each other. So, I guess out here is healthier, not that I could do it for long, Mr Lovely. Oh, I'd miss the buildings, you see. We've marvellous buildings. Palaces, cathedrals, gateways. Sometimes, I stand and wonder up at them. Our river, I reckon it's the best river in the world. I mean you call them rivers out here but they're no better than streams really, not wanting to be rude. " Then, "I think she was just answering a call. I can't see that she was out to meet anyone."

"Sounds to me that you don't know what to make of our village."

The truth was, Pepys didn't understand any of it. He was due to file his second report in the morning, but he had little to say. He had expected the pub, the Post Office and the path to the church to be good places to pick up gossip but he soon learned that he was too much the focus of village curiosity. Perhaps he would do better gaining the confidence of an individual informant. But the policeman,

Vicar and Verger were too old and too busy. He had been allowed to befriend the retired schoolmistress but, once again, found that she was good at listening but not fond of talking. (She thought that the fourteen year old was missing his mother.) So, he decided to cultivate one of the outsiders. The policeman's wife was unpopular but Pepys knew that, if he approached her, he would blush to his boots. The bespectacled Professor was more promising; he kept himself to himself but, when Pepys had given him thirty minutes that afternoon, he had been happy to talk. Now, the cellarman was saying that Pepys shouldn't give him any attention.

When the rain started, Pinch was standing beneath the churchyard elm, smoking his blackest tobacco in his largest pipe. The tobacconist in town called it Black Bull's Dung; he kept it under the counter and, whenever Pinch bought a fortnight's cache, the old shopkeeper repeated that he kept it for his especially esteemed customers. A summons to the Police Station was his only reason for going to town and he liked more than a week to pass between such visits. So he was careful not to run out of the heavy duty tobacco. But in spite of this restraint, the rich odour had become his signature. Even the village children could recognise it. Black Dung made more smoke than other mixtures. The night air made patterns with it and the drizzle made it sparkle. Pinch had often wondered about the properties of pipe smoke. He was sure that it brought special nutrients to plants when it stuck to the pale undersides of leaves. Last year, he had gone as far as allowing an ashtray of tobacco to smoulder beneath a garden shrub. It seemed to make no difference on that occasion but Pinch couldn't let go of the theory. He knew that tobacco was grown in hot countries; maybe he had tried his experiment in cold weather. "Can't discuss it with Meggastones," he whispered without taking the pipe stem from his lips. "Want to find the answers myself."

Pinch had been standing in the churchyard for more than an hour. He was neither bothered by the rain nor worried about the lateness of Peggy's return to the Police House. Her enticement of the Professor was the important first step in the recovery of the parish covenant and Pinch wanted it to go well.

He was quietly satisfied with himself whenever he manipulated his village and, that evening, Pinch had done some handsome police work. Seph Lovely had agreed to include Gus Becker in the skittles team. Whatever was going on behind the Beckers' closed door could only be resolved by the husband being encouraged to talk to the other men in the village, and Seph would make sure that those late night, light-headed conversations took place. Clemency Carstairs had taken measures to counter any worries that the new Vicar was harbouring about tomorrow's service and Doctor Dawes was already looking for evidence to strengthen the case against Macaulay.

His village was quiet. The Hornsbys had gone to bed and, just twenty minutes ago, the light at the Vicar's window had gone out. Edie Snag wasn't running around the village in her slippers that evening and Pinch had heard nothing of Mollie Sweatman since he had told her off and sent her home, half an hour ago. Seph Lovely had come to pray but he'd want to be out of the cold and the sparsely lit church before long. Yes, thought Pinch. All's well.

Then he saw the lamp shine from his own bedroom. Peggy was home and, he hoped, would have plenty to tell him. Pinch cleared his throat, laid the hot pipe in his coat pocket and started to tread his way across the damp grass towards the church path. But as he approached the kissing gate, he saw the bundle of clothes dumped by the low wall. He stood still and stared. He heard Lovely's heavy footsteps on the stone floor of the nave and, very faintly, the cabinet clock strike the half hour at the foot of the Vicarage stairs, but Pinch didn't take his eyes off the grey, lifeless shape. Not a bundle of clothes, he told himself. More like a body.

For a second, the thought stuck in his mind that a second murder counted for Macaulay's innocence. But then the more pressing present took over. He was about to walk through the long grass towards the body but stopped himself; the evidence of the grass might be important later on. So he marched quickly through the gate and, on the outside path, followed the dry stone wall. He was six yards off when he realised that the collapsed shape was Mollie Sweatman. He saw her hand reaching out from her sleeve; it had the horrid brownie-white colour of undercooked poultry. Just for a moment, he thought her blue neck moved but he told himself off for being gruesome. Pinch, she's dead.

But how?

He had hurried her towards home half an hour ago and he had followed her up the hill. Yes, he had lost sight of her when she reached the top green but surely he would have heard if she had been attacked. 'A skilful murderer, we've got,' but again he dismissed the thought in an instance. Observe, Pinch. Answer the questions the detectives will ask.

He leant over the wall and stretched out a hand until it touched her. He thought she moaned but at the same moment a big black bird flew out of the trees, screeching and flapping. Pinch twisted his neck to look, then had to reach out to stop himself falling to one knee.

"Watt yore doin!" Her head went back, her large brown eyes rolled and she sounded like a docker's penny whore.

Pinch gave a big sigh and put his weight on the top of the wall. "Grief Mollie, I thought you were ...."

"Knowed bloody well watt yore drinkin!" She rolled over and tried to raise herself to a crawl. She breathed in and held it.

"Thinking, Mollie," he corrected. "God, Mollie, you're drunk"

She said, still half-holding her breath, "Help me bloody up then!" and fell face down in the dirt.

Pinch clambered over the wall and took hold of her shoulders.

"Bloody off!" she yelled, as if he had woken her for the first time. "Bloody you!" She pushed herself up and backwards and would have laid herself flat but the wall saved her. "Bloody you! What do you know! Bloody policeman, think you do but you don't at all. You don't know —-" she shook her head more violently than she should have done. "—- anything!"

Pinch stepped back to a safe distance, then crouched down to her level. "Come on, Mollie. Let me take you home."

"What's your wife up to, Pinch? You don't know that, do you? Behind the Red Lion, she was, with the Professor and I heard what they were saying. You'd want to hear that, if you knew." Mollie wasn't sure that made sense. He watched her replay the words in her head, then shake them away. "She was telling him how he used to wait and watch for her at the school gates. And she said she enjoyed it, Mr Pinch. Enjoyed, another man watching her even though she was no more than a squint. I mean … squid? Squirt." She shook her head; that wasn't the word she wanted. "And I'll tell you what she made him promise. She's going to sneak in his Lodge tomorrow ev'ning, sneak in as if he doesn't know, and she's going to walk round and round so that he can take a good look at her, 'cept, you see … 'cept, he's got to pretend to be hiding and … " She tried to form the word. "… seeking." But she knew that wasn't what she meant to say either.

Pinch saw a light go on in the Vicarage. The Willowbys were already awake and making sure that their children kept the curtains closed. And Seth Lovely came striding out of the church and through the long wet grass. "Do you want me to help you carry her off, Constable," he called, determinedly. "I think we've all heard enough."

"I don't like him, Mr Pinch," Mollie said quietly in the policeman's ear. "I never have liked him."

Pinch placed a steadying hand on her arm.

"You shouldn't allow it, Pinch. Creating like some sort of harlot in the middle of the night."

"I'm not going to like him, Mr Pinch. He's always saying wicked things about Mollie."

Lovely had slowed down. Perhaps he saw something in her face, or perhaps he caught one too many of her whispered words. But he couldn't stop himself walking forward and, before he knew it, the man from the Red Lion had got too close.

"Prim arse!" she shouted.

Remembering it was the phrase Mollie had used about Peggy, Pinch hesitated for a crucial moment. The woman used his shoulder to steady herself, then threw a well aimed kick that sent Seth Lovely backwards, crouching and bawling. "The bitch! The little bitch!"

The excitement brought back the worst of her drunkenness. She started to wave her arms as she walked around in circles, calling out about two things at once. Everyone knew that she'd fall if she slowed down. Pinch tried to keep pace with her so that he could catch her when the moment came.

"I know what the trouble is," she cackled, turning to look at him. "You've got a weenie wallinger, and Peggy can't make ...." she tried two or three phrases before saying "... head nor tail of it. That's why she was in Mr Macaulay's bedroom, I think. I think she was Peking. Peeking. Peeping. Quinn. Pequin." She tossed her head. "She wanted to see if his wallinger was bigger than yours." She drew up a belch with so much power that she laughed at herself.

Then Verger Meggastones marched onto the scene. His bootlaces were undone, his hat was pulled down over his frozen ears and he wore an open raincoat over his pyjamas. "Having trouble here, Pinch?" Neither man knew if they were stronger rivals than friends. The Verger would not pass up an opportunity to present himself as the man who could sort things out when the old Dogberry couldn't.

Mollie shouted, "He's got a huge wallinger! I've seen it!"

"Right! She's needs locking up. Pinch, do your duty." Meggastones grabbed her wrist, Mollie reached for Pinch's elbow and they began to twirl in a dance of windmills sails.

"I caught him in the bushes and he had it out," Mollie sang. "Twice as big as any I've seen!"

Meggastones stood his ground but Mollie wouldn't release him and the three characters went down on their knees. Pinch's hands were in the mud, Meggastones was sitting in it and Mollie, seeing for the first time a tear in her dress, was trying to cry. She began to sing softly to herself, "Pom de pom de pom de pom-pom-da," and Pinch knew that 'Pinch has got a weenie wallinger' were the words in her head.

"My God, Pinch, what has she been at? No ordinary hooch does this!"

"I can't put her in the cell," Pinch explained. "If I do, I'll have to charge her. I can't shut women in the cell unless I charge them with something."

"But just to cool off, old man, surely."

But Pinch shook his head. "It's not the same case as a man," he explained. But he recognised that commonsense needed to override the rules. "Overnight, I suppose, and I'll leave the door open."

"Your cell? I'm not going in there!" Mollie decided indignantly. "I'm not being celled-up in Peggy Pinch's house. What sort of girl do you think I am? I have my pride."

"Then a ticket, Pinch," said the Verger. "Give her a ticket."

"What ticket?" Mollie asked, her eyes going from Meggastones to Pinch. Then, because that made her dizzy, they fixed on the ground.

"One of your tickets for the workhouse," the Verger insisted. "Pinch, anything will do."

"Good Lord, a removal ticket? I haven't used one in years. I'm sure I've still got the pad of forms somewhere but, Verger, I can't use them in a case like this. Mollie's already got a home to sleep in."

The cellarman came forward from the shadow of the church, where he had been recovering on some stone steps.

"Do you want to sleep on our hearth, Mollie?" he said.

Pinch and Meggastones said together. "In the Lion? You must be crazy."

They heard a garden gate open, halfway down The Street, and three lights were now shining from the Vicarage landing. "We'll have the whole village up here before long," the Verger warned. "They'll treat the whole thing like a circus."

"We've got to get the woman somewhere and, at least in the Lion, she'd know where she was." Pinch had pulled up clumps of grass and was wiping the mud from his hands. He couldn't understand why the man who had been so angry with her minutes before was now offering her his hearthrug. "Do you really think so, Lovely?"

Seth looked at the girl's face.

"I won't drop another touch," she promised, and no one corrected her.

But Meggastones threw in a spanner. "She wants to get at that youth, you've got."

Pinch sought the girl's word of honour. "Mollie?"

"No," Lovely said, still studying her expression. "Perhaps not."

Mollie had quietened down. She had withdrawn to the dry stone wall, where she picked at her fingers as she wept. When she thought the men weren't looking at her, she wiped her nose.

"Miss Carstairs, do you think?" suggested Pinch.

"We'd have a job getting her halfway down The Street," Meggastones warned. "Oh, God, look at the state of these pyjamas. I won't be able to sleep in these."

'Not as bad as my dress,' Mollie wanted to say, but she went on weeping instead. The episode began to feel like a game in the playground that had gone wrong and everyone was wary of going home. They were all in trouble.

"The police cell," Pinch decided. "I'll leave the door open and if there's no more trouble, you can leave before breakfast. What do you say, Mollie?"

The woman shrugged and pouted.

"You're quiet now, Mollie, but you've had too much to drink and who knows what you'd be like if you woke during the night."

She sighed heavily, pushed herself away from the wall and began a higgledy-piggledy walk towards the three men. Then she stopped, locked Meggastones in her sights, stepped forward and tapped his chest. "Mollie wants to sleep with you. You upstairs and me down. No, no. Me up and you down." She thought about it again, then nodded. Then nodded again to show that she was doubly sure.

"Ah no," said the Verger, visibly withdrawing. "No, no, no."

"I'll play up if we don't," she said mischievously. "We don't want Mollie to play up, do we, boys?"

Walking home alone, half an hour later, Pinch tried to make sense of Mollie's tell-tale on Peggy. He didn't doubt that his wife had been in Macaulay's bedroom some time before the murder. Mollie's gossip was so vicious that she couldn't risk it not to be true. And the revelation presented Pinch with a cute dilemma; if he persisted with his verbal evidence against Macaulay he risked making his wife a liar. But if he withdrew his statement (knowing that the confession he had pretended to hear was the only evidence against the suspect) Sergeants and Inspectors would be instructed to make his duties intolerable for years to come.

As he passed the War Memorial, lifting the peak of his cloth cap in respect, Queen O'Scots drifted forward from the shadows and walked with him to the garden gate. The cat picked up a sense that Pinch wasn't talking tonight but, he being a man and she being a cat, the silence made no difference to their companionship. She sat obediently at the garden gate, waited for him to pass through it, then watched him safely to the door. Two dead rabbits hung from the back door knob. A present from Poacher Baines, no doubt. (Pinch wasn't surprised that he had been able to get about the village without being noticed.)

"He's cleverer than us," he called out loud and Peggy, in bed, thought he was talking about the Professor.

CHAPTER NINE

Uneasy Prayers

This dawn was always going to be difficult. It came up clear with hardly a wind and nothing in the air to dampen the sounds of things waking. Before six, the Willowby children were up and dressed and standing at their front hedge. They were no nuisance but Mother thought that their idle waiting might be disrespectful so she called them in.

At ten to seven, Miss Carstairs pressed her gloves tightly over her fingers, adjusted her hat before the hall mirror and walked through to the kitchen for a last look around. She knew that Queen O'Scots had already taken up station on the front gatepost; this was unusual for Queenie generally watched from the Pinch's shed roof. Miss Carstairs decided that she was on the gate not to observe but to remind everyone that they had to be on time. This morning was so sensitive that everyone trod carefully. But the Beckers would still be late, Mollie Sweatman would be clumsy at the wrong moments and bird-like Edie Snag would be watching for signs that the village hadn't tried its best. There were good excuses for Mr Lovely to stay behind – the inn's back room would be crowded after the service – but Mr Lovely had a sound reason to be in Church from start to finish, so the landlady decided that they would go together but she would slip away early. No one needed to announce that folk would be welcome at the Vicarage for tea and a biscuit after the service or that others would muster in the Lion for a quarter of a round loaf, cheese and pickle, and ale to wash it down. Then, after the Vicar's house and the inn had emptied, Miss Carstairs would keep her door open for the half dozen women for whom this day was an ordeal from first light until the moment they closed their eyes for an afternoon's sleep. That was why she wanted Old School Cottage to be just right. Happy with her gloves, hat and kitchen, she checked that her handbag wasn't too full and stepped out of her front door.

Constable and Mrs Pinch were ready to leave. He wore his best tunic, the nap of his dress helmet had been perked up with a wire brush and, irregularly – because they weren't to be worn without permission – he had taken the starched white gloves from their cardboard box. Pinch was up to parade ground standard.

"Come on, Peggy," he said, because he saw that her face had weakened and that she was remembering the young men who had died. "We can't be late and I've already seen Miss Carstairs go up."

It had been Miss Carstairs' idea that there should be a special service each year on this morning. This was the day when the village post-boy had brought the news that fourteen of their young men had been lost in as many minutes. There had been a warning; three days before, the Master of the Grange had got word that the Pals had suffered dreadfully – but this was the morning when the families heard the names. Three other men would die before the War was over and everyone was remembered on Armistice Day but how could the village hear the sound of the post boy coming, year after year, on this date. Edie Snag had pleaded for something to be done. Miss Carstairs had argued that the morning delivery should be suspended for this one day, but apparently that couldn't be managed. So, a church service was designed to keep the parish together and busy during that awful breakfast time.

But, this year, the moment was uncanny. When the hymn finished but before the Vicar had started his speech and the congregation was standing in silence, they heard the post-boy on his round. His bicycle sounded like the wheels of execution. Little Edie, desperate not to cry, was shaking. Her hands gripped the back of the pew in front. Her head jerked on its neck and her knees wobbled. Mrs Willowby left her children and went to stand with her. Immediately, Edie slumped into her seat and she buried her head in her hands.

The Vicar caught the mood in an instant. Instead of commencing his address, he stood amongst his flock and bore with them the discomfort of the co-incidence of the post-boy. Together, they heard the Vicarage gate, the clap of a letter box in Wretched Lane and the youthful wail as the boy stuck his feet out from his pedals and free wheeled downhill.

There's preciousness in the moment when a clergyman recognises that he has been called to a flock. Throughout his schooling for the cloth, he had struggled with the concept of being blessed. His confused and lacking essays on the subject had become something of a joke between him and his teachers. But now, as he looked at the distressed faces before him, the Reverend saw clearly the path of his years to come. He thought, there could be few other moments in nature when a weight of responsibility is balanced by inner tranquillity. He was hardly aware of the service he delivered that morning. He started with the handwritten script but soon found himself drawing Nehemiah and Second Kings with insights that seemed to come from nowhere. Yet, this wasn't his moment – and it wasn't an occasion that the congregation wanted to hold. With compassion and confidence, he offered this gathering to those who hadn't returned.

The soldier boys were a lost generation and, when the peace came, the women found that there were no young men to marry. Ruby Becker and Peggy were assigned to older men, the young postmistress made a life with her brother and, in the years to come, the rascal that was Mollie Sweatman would be an old maid. As the 1920s grew longer and men of the War generation came to the village, the newcomers were talked about, they were celebrated, but the welcome was phoney and they'd leave within a twelvemonth. July 1916 was a wound that the village wouldn't fix.

The congregation dispersed in a sombre mood. There was no chatting on the church path, no wanting to be last, no reminders to share five minutes later on. When Pinch stood at the kissing gate, watching his wife walk alone down the front street, he had an uncomfortable feeling that more than one distance was lengthening between them.

He had no doubt that Mollie's drunken meanderings had grown out of her knowledge of the murder scene. Pinch looked at Miss Carstairs, the new Vicar, Doctor Dawes and the group from the Red Lion, and he wondered what these people would say about a policeman's wife who had climbed a neighbour's stairs to watch Tug Macaulay in his bed.

Seth Lovely broke away from the little group and trudged towards him. "I just want to say, Pinch, that I'll always be grateful for Master Thomas from Back Lane." He had no particular reason to say this to the policeman but Pinch engaged him. Nodding, tentatively offering a hand, keeping to one side so that Seth could simply walk away without being discourteous. "They say he was never born for soldiering but he kept the lads together even as he went down with them. It's a comfort, it is, knowing that Robert would have felt that someone familiar was in charge during his last moments."

Mollie was being lectured by the Vicar at St Stephens' porch. Otherwise, the churchyard had emptied. Pinch led Seth Lovely through the gate and stayed with him for a dozen or so steps down The Street. Then he held back and let the poor man continue alone.

"May I explain?"

Pinch turned and saw a penitent Mollie Sweatman at his shoulder. She stood, round shouldered and flat footed, with her hands held in front of her and her face drained of any colour.

"I think not," he replied. "I think not."

She bit her lip and withdrew from his sight, only to be replaced by the Reverend. "I put her on her word of honour not to repeat what she said," he said quietly.

Pinch was looking at the freshly prepared, spotless church robes that moved gently in the morning breeze; the Vicar seemed at ease in them. He was holding his Parson's Pocketbook lightly in one hand. The church bell began to ring.

"I couldn't help but hear the rumpus last night," the Vicar said quietly, dipping his head and taking half a step backwards. "Please, don't imagine that I was eavesdropping. But, don't you see, Pinch, the danger for Peggy."

"I see very well," Pinch assured him, unaware that he had brought his pipe from his trouser pocket. He caught sight of it and put it away; he didn't want the village to spot him smoking in his Number Ones.

"I wasn't thereabouts when poor Miss Wells was killed," the Vicar was saying. "But I've asked a good many questions. The killer wasn't seen running up or down The Street, so we have all assumed that he was hiding in one of the cottages, and that has to be Old School Cottage. But, if Mollie is telling us the truth…"

"Yes, I see very well," Pinch repeated.

"Pinch, no one can believe that your wife was in another man's bedroom. It's nonsense. But she was in Miss Carstairs' kitchen for longer than might be thought reasonable. And once that is recognised."

"You're saying that if the murderer didn't run up or down The Street and wasn't hiding upstairs in Old School Cottage, he must have escaped along the garden's side path."

"If Peggy was in the kitchen, she would have seen him," the Reverend concluded. "You must warn her. It may be that Seth Lovely, the Verger and I weren't the only ones to hear Mollie's outburst. It may be that the murderer heard it all."

"My wife and I need to talk." The sentiment sounded like a good step forward.

The Vicar smiled; he offered best wishes.

Pinch, now feeling out of place in his best dress, waited at the War Memorial. He watched the Vicar make for Edie Snag's Bulpit Cottage but, at the last moment, he was called back to the Verger's garden gate. The Willowby children had already changed into everyday clothes and Driver David was turning the village bus at the top of The Street.

Then, in one image, Pinch caught the schoolma'am's cat, the Postmistress and the Becker boy looking at him from different directions and he felt that the whole village had heard Mollie Sweatman's naughty gossip. Man and wife would be talking about it. Children would be told not to mention what they couldn't understand but brothers and sisters would still whisper to each other when they were alone. Before long, Pinch would catch conversations that stalled in mid-sentence and neighbours would want to deny the inquisitive looks on their faces. Nosy Parkers would be tasked to mark any unusual deliveries or visitors to the Police House, or times when the Vicar or Doctor stayed with the Pinches for too long. The over sixties, who considered themselves village worthies, would be looking for moments when they could take Pinch to one side.

Peggy and Pinch needed to talk.

He straightened his helmet and stepped smartly towards home, already rehearsing the first words he would say to her. He didn't like to rebuke her – it seemed to emphasise their age difference – and Pinch was always aware that it would be too easy for him to bully her. Generally, Peggy knew when she was in the wrong and, when she didn't, Pinch had developed a look that could put her there without a word. Sometimes, she needed a stern remark or an inflection in his tone to keep her in line, but where was the woman who didn't? This time, Peggy had let herself down. She had allowed her silly thinking to get the better of her and it was Pinch's job to bring her down to size. 'Have her standing in the middle of the carpet, Pinch. No fidgeting and her eyes downcast while you brace yourself in front of the hearth.' He puffed and panted as he marched through the garden gate. 'Nothing too much, Pinch. Your Peggy won't need more than one of two Sergeant-type reps. Then dismiss her.'

But he had yet to reach the porch step when Peggy fell out of the front door, one hand holding her hat on her head, the other trying to close her handbag.

"Oh! Pinch, yes." She looked over his shoulder at the bus waiting at the War Memorial. "Yes. No!" She waved her hand. "I'll miss the bus. Gosh, Pinch, I need to ... oh, Lord, you're cross with me now."

"Peggy, go back indoors?"

"Oh, Pinch," she pleaded. "Don't say that. A letter has come and I really must go." She dug an envelope from her handbag and pressed it into his hands. "Pinch, the bus, please."

Her husband took his time. He studied the envelope, unfolded the notepaper and brought his pipe to his mouth before reading. "Driver David has seen that you are hurrying," he mumbled without looking at her. "He won't leave without you."

They were standing together beneath their front porch, Peggy hopping from one foot to the other, Pinch grim-faced as he read the letter.

"I know I'm due a telling off, Pinch, and I don't want to get away with it but …"

"Yes," he agreed, tapping his pipe-stem on the notepaper. "You must attend to this on your own. I shall telephone Sergeant Haynes, just to look out for you. I'll give him no details, of course. Yes, quickly now, off you go."

PART THREE

CHAPTER TEN

A Little Mischief in a Tea Shop

Driver David called out the news as he steered the twenty-five seater through the country lanes at less than fifteen miles an hour. The miners were likely to settle. One of the film stars had died but he didn't know who. Two musicians in the town's dance band had been taken by the revenue men in the middle of a performance; he thought it was something to do with drink. David's audience didn't respond. The husband and wife from the house at the ford were seated in the middle seats but weren't talking. Mrs Hornsby looked out the window from beginning to end. And Peggy was too busy thinking about the strange letter that had been delivered to the Police House. It had been written in the tone of a secret message, so she guessed that the editor of the Cheriton Call knew nothing about it. Probably, the journey had cost Miss Duffle not only the train fare but also a day's holiday. Peggy concluded that the boy Pepys was in serious trouble.

By the time the bus reached the first houses of the market town, a horrible grinding noise at the back had grown so loud that the women believed that they could smell it. Driver David seemed worried about the heat rising from under his seat. Everyone was holding tight and, creeping along at a walking pace, the coach finished its journey by freewheeling on the forecourt of Badger Motor Engineers. "A bit of dusting and polish will see her right," David promised. "She'll be on the square twenty minutes before you're all ready to go back." No one spoke to Peggy as they filed off the bus.

Sergeant Haynes stood at the Buttercross and watched Peggy cross the broad street. "Good morning, Mrs Pinch." He saluted courteously. "I shall be here on the hour if you'd like a car to take you home. Arthur didn't think you'd want to wait for the afternoon bus."

"That's very kind of you, Sergeant."

No one else recognised her and she hurried along the pavement, uninterrupted. Past Townsend's Bicycles (Makers and Repairers), Thornton's Lamps, Wicks and Candles, and on to the street corner dominated by a family poulterer. Fresh meat hung over the pavement from rows of timber beams. The display was decorated with greenery and brought so much attention that passers-by had to step into the road. Peggy remembered a childhood visit when she had been fascinated by a bluff gentleman, in a tall hat and a white smock, who used a high hooking pole to bring the plucked birds down from the higher levels. Today, she didn't stop to look but was brought up at the kerb when two opposing motorists arrived at the corner simultaneously. They were bumper to bumper and neither knew what to do. As Peggy crossed behind them, she saw Sergeant Haynes take up position in the middle of the High Street. He made an importance of stopping the traffic.

A bell rattled unevenly on its spring as she entered the tea shop. Mrs Hornsby was on the pavement, studying the menu in the window. When she saw that Peggy had walked in, she tutted, clasp her handbag to her bosom and walked off.

The tables were busy. Ladies, sitting on their own or in pairs, occupied their regular corners, and shoppers with baskets got in the way of others in the middle. The couple from the house at the ford were sharing tea and buns, and a post-lady was in the middle of her morning break. There were two dogs and one empty cat-basket. A parrot in a tall cage had been lodged on the counter for safe keeping. It was, thank goodness, a very quiet parrot. A retired officer, in tweeds and brogues, was working on the crossword and, every now and then, stepped across to the post-lady for advice. The young waitress in a black dress and white apron, who seemed to know what she was doing although no one else could work it out, tried to draw Peggy to an undesirable table for one, next to the till, but Miss

Duffle raised her hand and coo-eed in a manner that went well with the general commotion of the place.

"Mrs Pinch, I'm pleased you have come."

"How did you recognise me?"

"Oh, my dear, the puzzled look on your face."

In another corner, the black and white girl had delivered a slice of cake to the wrong table. The disgruntled customer muttered condemnation and tapped the handle of a knife on the table cloth. The waitress apologised, smiled politely and withdrew without turning her back, but all her training made no difference. The grump went on muttering.

"I don't have long," said Peggy. Without a sound, she mouthed 'one tea' at the waitress who accepted the order with a nod as she tended to the correct customer and his cream cake.

"Of course." Miss Duffle pushed her plate aside and showed she wanted nothing to do with her cup of tea. "Mrs Pinch, I have read Pepys's letters to the office and, since he has been away, I have found his journal. Mrs Pinch, I am very concerned about things. I didn't have time to explain in my letter, so let me tell you how things are."

But it was Peggy who started the story. "Pepys' mother is Tillie Lovely who used to live in Bulpit Cottage, before little Edie Snag took it over. Tillie left the village when she realised that she was pregnant. Partly, that was due to a great argument with Seth, her father, but perhaps she would have been right to move anyway. She took a new name. She might be married, no one in the village knows. No one is sure how well she knew your employer, Mr Hardcastle. He had visited the village as a school inspector, and it may be that there had been some sort of falling out with Seth. Over what, no one says. However, Hardcastle must have kept an eye on our Tilly because he gave her son his first job. Maybe he settled some money for the boy's upbringing?"

"All this is common knowledge in your village?" Miss Duffle asked.

"Probably. But in bits and pieces rather than the whole."

Miss Duffle smiled at Peggy's way of putting it.

"Miss Carstairs, who we call our schoolmistress though she retired some years ago – it must irritate our young teacher, but there it is – Miss Carstairs would know absolutely all there is to know but she keeps it very quiet."

"Ah, Miss Carstairs. Of course, she still has her cat. Richard III?"

"She has Queen O'Scots now."

"But she used to have two. Richard III and John of Gaunt."

Peggy smiled at the memory of the two pets who used to wander in and out of her childhood classroom.

"And neither of them a Tom," said Miss Duffle.

Peggy hadn't known that. "I always assumed …" she began.

"Love was so unkind to Miss Carstairs. Of course, you will think that Cedar was cruel to place herself in your village, but I saw both sides of the matter. Your village probably sees Cedar Wells as a vengeful and deceitful woman but I want to tell you that she was nothing like that. She cared for others and put herself last. Cedar was patient with Mr Hardcastle's little love affairs. When poor Tilly appeared, carrying his child, she was so kind to her. Mr Hardcastle always looked after the child, we all know that, but Cedar was the woman who wouldn't let him turn his back on them."

"You've no doubt that Hardcastle is Pepys' father?"

"No doubt at all, Mrs Pinch. That's why I say that Cedar was a good woman. She suffered it all with dignity. And when she found out that he had a secret true love – your old school teacher – she was heartbroken, but never angry or vengeful. She came to our office one afternoon when Mr Hardcastle hadn't been seen for days and she sobbed in front of me. Mrs Pinch, she cried like I have seen no one cry. She left him because she knew that she couldn't bear to hold only part of his heart. That was the difference, she told me; she had always known that his little fancies meant nothing to him, but your Miss Carstairs meant the world to him. I remember her saying to me that a wronged wife deserves the last laugh. You see, it was always Mr Hardcastle's hope that he could return to your village and Miss Carstairs but, with Cedar placed between them, so to speak, it was quite impossible."

"Aren't those the thoughts of a vengeful wife, Miss Duffle?"

"No, not in the end. In the end, Cedar realised that he would only hurt your Miss Carstairs. I'm sure she told her that. They were fond of each other in the end, you know. Your Miss Carstairs and my Cedar. Tell me, does Mr Willowby still tend his front garden so carefully?"

"How do you know so much about our little place, Miss Duffle."

"Because your schoolmistress has written to me over the years and when my editor is half asleep and three quarters drunk, and too lonely to go home, he dreams aloud. I can't say, but perhaps that is how young Pepys learned some of the history. I think he has no idea that Mr Hardcastle was his father but it seems that the young boy has picked up an idea that Cedar Wells was standing in the way of his mother and father marrying and making a home for the three of them."

"This is in his journal?"

Mrs Duffle nodded. "Who knows? Pepys is such a simple lad. I'm sure he will have mixed things up. But who knows what goes on in a boy's head?"

"But this makes no difference. The murder happened before Pepys came to our village. He can't possibly have done it."

The waitress was clearing the next table. Peggy noticed her sweep the three ha'pence tip into the pocket of her apron with a speedy simplicity that was almost sleight of hand. A retired gentleman by the window beckoned her by gently raising one hand and, in one smooth movement, she delivered the tray to the counter, collecting a saucer of three biscuits, and had her pencil and pad ready before she reached the table in the bay.

"We all thought that he was poorly at home for three days that week," Duffle was saying. "But I have spoken to his mother and, no, he had told her he was staying with a young uncle in town."

"And the uncle knows nothing about it?"

"It's some months since he has heard from Pepys."

"Then he has a motive for murder and no alibi."

"He's such a young lad, Mrs Pinch. We must be able to do something for him."

"Miss Duffle, why have you told me this? You know I'm the village policeman's wife and I can't keep from him anything you tell me."

"Because Pepys says you're the only one who would understand about the windows."

"I'm afraid I don't know what he's talking about," said Peggy but her words were lost in a hub-bub. Suddenly the Copper Kettle was busy. An auction had been completed at the lace stall in the market square and an excited needle circle was bubbling over with news of their losses and gains. They would have preferred three adjacent tables and the rest of the cafe had to put up with order and counter-order until the sewing club accepted that it wasn't practicable to have their own corner. Peggy decided that she didn't really like women who lived in towns.

Miss Duffle must have said something to excuse herself because the next thing Peggy knew, the woman was walking off to the cloakroom. Peggy sat alone and, as her mind replayed the woman's words, her skin went cold; she realised that the conversation had taken her one step towards identifying Cedar Wells' killer. "I don't want to say so," she said quietly as she gathered her handbag and gloves. "but, yes, the most important clue so far."

During the confusion, haughty Mrs Hornsby had come into the shop and seated herself in a dark corner with her back to Peggy. In a delicious moment, Peggy realised that the woman could not have seen her. She got to her feet, bowed her head away from the company, and kept her fingers hidden deep in her handbag as she walked quickly towards the thin door that let the waitress into the kitchen. As Peggy passed behind Mrs Hornsby she seemed to sway precariously towards her but even those tea-drinkers who saw her paid little attention.

The woman shot to her feet, shrieking and flapping like a stuck bird. "A mouse! I can feel a mouse!" She began to twirl in circles, trying to catch up with her back, as a dozen women came to her aid. A chair toppled over. A table cloth slid to a table's edge and the waitress waited for the crash of cups and saucers (but they survived). "It's down my back!" shouted Mrs Hornsby, then she let out an outrageous scream that brought Sergeant Haynes running from the market place.

A twelve year old in short trousers was kneeling on the table, trying to hold her shoulders still as he put his hand down the collar of her coat. "Can't feel a moussie. Can't feel nothing crawlie down 'ere."

"Young man! Whatever do you think you are doing!" Mrs Hornsby's shoulders were pushed forward as the boy groped, and the collar of her dress felt ready to choke her. "Young man! Young man! What do you think you are doing!"

"Reaching for the moussie, Mrs. You can never tell how far down these scallies get."

"Young man!"

The proprietor ran into the shop, wiping his hands on his dirty white apron. "No creature's come from my kitchen. How could it? How could a dead mouse run from my kitchen and up your dress." The notion of things running up dresses caused many customers to retreat. An old gentleman tried to rub his ankles together while he stood still, as if he were trying to close off his trouser legs.

"Ha!" yelled the lad, producing the mouse by its tail with all the glee of Jack Horner pulling out his plum. He threw it into the air, everyone screamed some more and the proprietor demanded its capture.

"Now then," growled the Police Sergeant, shutting the front door behind him and righting a chair. "I can't believe you lot are causing trouble in here. What's it all about?"

Mist seemed to clear from Mrs Hornsby's eyes. "Has that Pinch-wife been in here?"

"There!" declared the owner triumphantly. "Sergeant, a brown mouse! How could that be when we have only white mice in our kitchen!"

Peggy had left the tea-house by a side door and found herself in a damp and dingy side road, where a stray mongrel was half in an upturned dustbin and tall brick walls kept out the light. She was tickled by the excitement she had left behind but knew that the moment wouldn't last. Her head was full of new things. Not knowing where she was suited the mood. The revelation that young Pepys might have been in the village before the murder and that Miss Carstairs' lost love might be his father made trivia of all her previous thoughts about Cedar's death. Slowly, she stepped towards the daylight of the market place and stood at the kerb while she recovered her bearings.

At the Buttercross, the town's friendly radical was denouncing Baldwin. The show-off was dressed in hideous yellow tweed. He had a cloth cap bunched in one hand, while he jabbed the other's forefinger in the air. The lady from the bakery delivered a paper parcel of hot buns; he nodded a thank you as she set it at his feet, but he didn't allow her to interrupt his flow. Sergeant Haynes, having left the rioters in the teashop and taken up station at the greengrocer's junction, was content to let the fellow chant his slogans – after all, many in the town agreed with his arguments and those who didn't chose to smile rather than challenge him.

Haynes was cheerfully overweight. He would have been more comfortable with his helmet pushed back from his brow and the polished buttons loosened at the neck of his heavy tunic – yes, he'd look good as a laughing policeman – but he set to his duties with undiluted discipline. He watched before commenting. He stepped away so that he could take a broad view of things rather than an urgent observation. He had a finely developed knack of placing himself in the right spot of a pavement so that others would approach and talk to him. (Something that Pinch couldn't do, Peggy reflected. Pinch had to be part of things, or walk away.)

"What's been going on in the Kettle?" asked one old woman.

"Nought but a bunch of kiddies," growled the Sergeant. "They're best left to it."

Peggy was crossing the broad street – busy with handcarts, pedestrians, motor vehicles and walking farm-stock – before she noticed that Doctor Dawes had parked his new car outside the chemist's shop. She was just a few yards from the motor, not really looking where she was going in spite of the traffic, when the crowd gave the speaker a louder than normal cheer. Peggy nearly joined in;

she didn't know what 'Imperial Preference' meant but she knew that it sounded good. It put the Empire first, she guessed.

Dawes was laughing. He was holding two bags of heavy shopping close to his chest, "You'd welcome a lift home?" he asked.

"Oh, that would be kind!" She was a little uneasy because the Doctor would deliver her to the village earlier than Pinch expected; but it all seemed innocent enough.

The Doctor stowed his shopping in the back, then walked around the car to open the passenger door and help Peggy into her seat. From the start, she felt that she shouldn't be in the cramped little car. It wasn't built for ladies; ladies carried too much that might get in the way of the driver. She balanced her handbag on her thighs, tucked her elbows in and kept her knees together. Folds of the coat seemed to be everywhere and untidy, and she didn't know where she was supposed to rest the heels of her shoes.

With a disturbing clank of pedals and levers, the Doctor got the car into gear. "Right-ho! Off we go."

The main road was jammed by a score of cows, being driven by a lad no older than ten. The town's second Constable directed the car down a side street, which the Doctor seemed pleased about.

"It means protecting British goods," he shouted. "The Imperial Preference. Keeping imports out or taxing them heavily."

Peggy didn't know what to say. Then she remembered Pinch's opinion of the Prime Minister and said, "I like Mr Baldwin. I always think that a quiet man has a lasting strength." (She hoped she'd got the phrase right.)

He drove through an open railway crossing and into the countryside.

Peggy let her elbows squeeze her ribs. She didn't like travelling in cars. A good strong cart would go only where the horse thought it was safe to lead. The wheels and engine of a motorcar would go, without question, where a man directed; that didn't make a safe basis for getting along country lanes.

"I usually race that loco driver," the Doctor shouted with a nod at the puffer, two fields away. "But not when you're with me."

"Please. I don't mind."

But Dawes knew she wouldn't feel safe. "It takes less than twenty minutes if I cut over the Edge."

They passed familiar landmarks. The rough meadow where she had picnicked as a child. The old mill pond where two school-friends had drowned. The broken wooden fence where she liked to rest and watch the ponies.

"You love your car, Doctor," she remarked simply.

"But, oh, a guilty pleasure, I'm afraid. I got it far too cheaply and now some gentlemen are offering me a handsome price. Do you think I should sell it and share the profit with Mrs Thurrocks?"

"Not at all. She was very keen that you should have it, for all the help that you gave her husband over the years. No, I'm sure she'd want you to keep it. We'd all be sorry to see it leave the village."

"Perhaps you are right."

"Doctor, may I ask you something?"

"Please, do."

"On the day Cedar died, you gave Miss Carstairs a lift to town. Did she stay with you? I mean, did you bring her back."

"No, she was too busy and I especially wanted to get back for Mrs Jenner."

"Only."

"Yes?"

"Only, Edie Snag has told me that Miss Carstairs was back early, as well. She visited Bulpit Cottage and spoke about the library."

He opened his mouth to speak, checked his memory, then shook his head. "No. Definitely. Edie's got it muddled, I'm certain."

The car was rattling rather than chugging or churning. The mechanics can't be sound, Peggy thought, and she gripped the straps of her handbag.

"Peggy, my dear, it will save time if you allow me to breach a confidence. You are not the only one asking questions about Miss Carstairs and the morning of the murder. Our Vicar has been to see me; he asked me to approach our old schoolma'am about something he's heard. Something, he's been told. "

"Who by?"

"No, that doesn't matter. The issue is, someone heard Edie Snag say that Miss Carstairs knew the truth ..."

"About what?"

"Well, no one's quite sure. Miss Carstairs herself can make no heads or tails of it, but Edie quite clearly said that Miss Carstairs knew all about it and would show everyone at half past eleven on Friday. You see ... "

"The moment when Cedar was killed. Doctor, you must tell me who overheard the remarks."

"That would be quite wrong of me. You see, even our Vicar wasn't sure how to handle it. That's why he came to me and asked my advice. He said that I'd known Miss Carstairs for a long time and he wanted me to talk to her, to clear things up."

"And?"

"Well, it could be nonsense. She cannot think what Edie meant."

"But even if it's nonsense, it is important nonsense. Someone must speak to Edie."

"That, Mrs Pinch, is my very next step."

They passed the Wishing Stone, a granite intrusion that looked out from The Edge. Children said that the stone was magic because it was the discarded knuckle from a dinosaur's toe. The Professor always offered an astrological explanation and persuaded many villagers that, on six nights each year, its spirit could be felt at preordained compass points in the parish. Peggy had never believed that, but the Wishing Stone was sometimes called the Witch's Stone and she couldn't make up her mind if the silver and blue veins had been blessed by good or bad fairies.

"Is this your first time in a man's car?" he asked.

"Of course not," she insisted and began to count the occasions in her head. She got as far as twenty and was about to ask if cars included buses when she recognised his emphasis on 'a man's car'. Of course, all cars belonged to men (at least, all cars that Peggy knew about) but the Doctor meant 'alone with a man in a car'.

"Please, don't feel uncomfortable," he was saying. "I had to reassure dear Cedar that a Doctor can speak as no other fellow can. All her play-acting as a chap, it left her wanting, you know. That's why I suggested an arrangement between us. An arrangement that allowed us to behave in an intimate way. Always, a business arrangement; there was never deceit. My dear Peggy, it's an arrangement that I'm able to propose between us, you and I. I know all things aren't as they should be in your marriage."

His words were so unexpected, yet delivered so naturally, that Peggy had to digest them before she could make sense of them. By then, the Doctor was talking about Widow Jenner's condition, emphasising how genuinely concerned he was.

Peggy kept quiet, but she boiled at the man's arrogance. He felt safe making such a horrid suggestion because he knew that, if she spoke up, no one would believe her or, if they did, she would be charged with being flighty and encouraging.

"Peggy, we'll say no more at the moment, but you must keep it in mind." He nodded. "We'll talk again."

Peggy resolved not to speak for the rest of the journey. She chewed her lip, she quirked her nose and breathed in deeply. She twisted her fingers in the straps of her handbag and squirmed in her seat until it got too much for her. When they reached the top of the Edge and the Doctor's hand slipped from the steering wheel and caressed the knob of the gear stick, she spat out "Twenty two!" And, "that's not including the bus two or three times a month."

The smug look on the Doctor's face said that Peggy's tetchiness was understandable and, really, there was no need for him to respond. Just very slightly, he nodded, and the knots in Peggy's stomach felt worse. She promised that she would do something (but she knew that she wouldn't). She would talk to Miss Carstairs (but not for a long time and then she would insist that the matter couldn't be mentioned to others). Well, if she couldn't challenge the Doctor, she would find another way of getting her own back. She would decide on a trick. A childish one, maybe, but a prank that couldn't be easily recovered and one that would leave him in no doubt that more was to come.

The Doctor stopped the car at the church green, where The Street, Back Lane and Wretched Lane come together. "Would it be awfully …" he began.

"Not at all," she said sharply. "I shall be very happy to walk from here. I've noticed how much you prefer to use the stony roads rather than The Street." She was out of the car, and slammed the door before the Doctor could lean over and close it gently. "I do hope, Dr Dawes, that you break your neck before very much longer."

No doubt, he gained some satisfaction from her petulance, but if she didn't look back she need never know.

"Blasted men," she grumbled quietly as she walked down the road. "Blast them all. The Doctor wants me to betray my husband, my husband wants me to parade in front of the Professor, and the Professor wants to look at my legs when I walk up his stairs. Almighty knows what the Vicar wants and since God knows all things, I shan't ask him."

But she stopped in her tracks. The Post Office was closed, the Willowby curtains were drawn and a stranger's car was parked on the patch of grass where the path to Widow Jenner's house joined The Street. She read the signs; she turned away from the Police House but immediately felt a tug on her sleeve.

"This won't make any difference, Mrs Pinch?" The Professor had been waiting for her. He looked damp and cold.

"I promised," Peggy retorted shortly. "I said ten o'clock. Now, get away from me."

CHAPTER ELEVEN
Two Deaths

Sheets and towels, soaked with blood, had been dumped from the widow's back door, ready for burning. In the kitchen, Miss Carstairs was dressed for action and scrubbing everywhere with soda. She worked from three huge bowls. Her forearms and hands were red.

"It didn't go well?" said Peggy, looking around, wanting to help immediately but at a loss.

"We got Doctor Johnny over from St Faiths."

Peggy nodded. "Dr Dawes was in town." It wasn't his fault, she wanted to say. "The Professor, he was outside, waiting in The Street."

"Peggy?"

"It's …" She shook her head. "It's nothing. Just something, Pinch said. The Professor would be on hand, he said, if …"

Miss Carstairs kept looking at the door to the parlour; she didn't want people to hear.

"But Postmistess Mary? She was here for her?" asked Peggy

"By the time she arrived, it was all over. It seems that our new Vicar saw the whole thing through. He's done it before. He delivered his own son last year."

Too quickly, Peggy said, "But the maid says there's no child." Then she read the schoolma'am's face and the words, dry and forced, seemed to scratch their way from the back of her mouth. "Oh, the poor man."

"Ruby Becker has taken in the little mite."

Peggy felt her eyes flinch involuntarily. Everyone knew that the

Becker household was troubled; surely, the Willowbys would have been a better sanctuary for the new-born.

"He seems strong enough," Miss Carstairs was saying. "But Mrs Jenner's exhausted. Doctor Johnny says … he's talking as if … he means she'll be lucky to get through it without an infection." She added, "Postmistress Mary won't give in. She's been upstairs for hours."

Peggy couldn't remember seeing her old schoolmistress so drained. She said, "Give me a few minutes. I'll get home, leave something out for Pinch's tea, then I'll take over."

Miss Carstairs was shaking her head. "Pinch thinks you might do the nightshift, but we're not to count on you before ten. You've a job to do, or something?"

Peggy felt a deep anger well in her chest. All this, and the men wanted to persist with their silly game. They had worked up a plan and would allow nothing to spoil it.

"He says you needn't bother with his tea. I think he'll sit down for something at the Red Lion. Peggy, if you want to help, you could sit with the Vicar for a few minutes." She nodded towards the parlour. "I know you'll do well."

He was sitting in the armchair where Mabel Jenner liked to read and knit. He looked exhausted. He tie was loose, his collar undone. His cropped black hair was sticking up where he had run his hands. He was slouched to one side and his large hands were wrapped around his face. Peggy knelt on the floor beside the chair and shifted until she was comfortable.

"I mustn't sit here," he said softly. "I'll be needed upstairs before long, Johnny says, but he insisted I should take a rest. I'm sorry, I mean Doctor Johnny."

Peggy smiled. She knew it was best to say nothing. She moved a little, letting him know that she was ready to take his hand, but he didn't want it.

"I've let her down," he said.

"No, Vicar. We've all let her down. We've been too concerned with other things, these last few days. Our silly prattle and sneaking about." Then, thinking of her prank with the dead mouse, she added, "Our silly games."

She stayed at his feet. The soft lighting helped their burdened souls draw closer together. With her face down, she found that her eyes had fixed on the fraying folds of his turn-ups.

"Your husband is a good citizen, Mrs Pinch." She felt his fingertip rest on her shoulder. "He has a pamphlet by a man called Herbert."

"I'm sure he'd want to lend it to you."

He managed a half smile. "No, I've read Herbert's works many times. He wrote about all the things a country parson should be. This morning has made me think that I should pay greater attention to his stricture, but half of me knows I will never be good enough."

"Nonsense. People are saying how good you'll be. This morning's service was lovely. You mustn't be alone in the vicarage tonight. I'll speak with Pinch. I'm sure he won't mind my taking your guest room."

"I shan't be alone," he replied simply.

"I know your maid has her own room with you but that hardly counts as company." A Vicar could hardly share sherry with his maid.

"I have sent my wife a telegram. She hopes to be here before supper."

"No. Surely she needs to stay with your father-in-law?"

"Isabelle agrees that our parish must come first. She trained as a nurse during the War. She'll be able to sit with the Willowby child."

The light flickered and the gas spluttered as it forced its way through some debris in the lamp.

"I don't understand," said Peggy. "I haven't heard. I've been in town all morning."

"Grace Willowby has the scarlet fever."

"Oh, dear God, no." Peggy buried her face in her hands so that, in moments, her tears ran through her fingers. She heard herself repeating, "No, no, no."

"Doctor Johnny is arguing that she should be isolated at home. That's what the Willowbys want. Isabelle's training will make sure that the quarantine is respected."

"Oh, poor Grace."

"Young Gary will be dispatched to his grandparents."

"Dear God, what's happening to us?"

"Our Father wishes us to come together. Each one of us must resolve our differences with our neighbours so that we can receive the full strength of his fellowship."

How misplaced the dead mouse seemed now. The villagers would be angry when they heard of it. Already, she could hear the women muttering behind their hands.

"You must settle matters with young Mollie Sweatman," the Vicar said quietly. "She is very fond of you, Peggy. She would want you to think of the time at the Wishing Pool."

Peggy throat clenched, forcing her face red and making her head swim. What had the little minx told him? She imagined her hinting, just enough for the Vicar to gather a good idea of what had gone on that night. Peggy Pinch hated Mollie Sweatman. Hated her. She managed to press little quick breaths into her mouth; she was sure she was going to faint. The gas mantel was ready to expire – its hiss and spitting making Peggy think that the room was gasping for air.

Then Miss Carstairs stepped into the room. "Mary wonders if you might …"

"Yes, yes." He got to his feet and, as silently as only Vicars can move, he left the two women alone.

"She says it won't be long," Miss Carstairs reported to Peggy. "No more than a matter of minutes. She has lost so much blood, you see." She sat on the floor with her friend.

"We failed her," Peggy said. "We've had our minds on other things. Each one of us has left her for someone else."

"What has happened couldn't be helped."

"I hate this village. I hate the people who live in it and the look of all the houses and the way the lanes turn on themselves."

"Nonsense, dear."

"I hate myself more than anything."

"Now, Peggy, none of us deserve self pity at a time like this." She placed her fingers on the back of Peggy's hand, and they both listened for any clue of matters upstairs. Postmistress Mary was carrying empty flasks to the top of the staircase. Someone else was opening a window. A death in a house brings its own hollowness, thought Miss Carstairs.

"I don't know how Mollie Sweatman knows, but the story she's putting about is true. She's right, Miss Carstairs, I did creep up your staircase. I opened his bedroom door and when I saw that the sheets and blankets were screwed up around him, I went further. I walked in, because I wanted to see him open to the air." Peggy was saying more than she had intended but now that she was telling the truth, it became easier to say it all. "I wanted to see how different he was from Pinch."

There. The words were out.

Peggy fell silent. Later, she would find time enough for weeping but kneeling on the widow's carpet with a neighbour she had known since childhood provided a comfort that she didn't want to disturb. At first, Miss Carstairs seemed to make little of the confession. Perhaps her old schoolteacher was turning over the words in her mind, perhaps she was waiting for more. "You must tell no one else." The advice came quietly, with no judgement besides a common sense way forward. "Whatever Mollie says, no matter how strong her accusations, you must always deny what you have just told me."

"No, I must face what I've done."

"Then you'll never be free of it, and Pinch will be broken." She added, "Broken, for everyone to see."

"I take my wedding vows seriously, Miss Carstairs."

"I know that, dear."

"And I have done something very wrong. I am guilty."

As she walked from Widow Jenner's cottage to the Police House, she passed the grass where Mollie had been standing an hour before. The verge was empty now, but Peggy knew that the woman would return. Perhaps the blackmail was done with, but Peggy's best enemy would want to cause more mischief. "How did she know?" Peggy repeated to herself as she crossed the village street.

She wanted Pinch to hear her coming. She rattled the front gate, pretended that the mat was caught behind the kitchen door, and made a great fuss of changing her shoes as soon as she was indoors. She noticed the familiar sounds of her home; the click of a Welsh dresser cupboard that fell open whenever the back door was opened and the hem of the kitchen curtain tapping against the timber frame. These, like the four second dribble of cold water from the brass tap, were almost a welcome home. She noticed the odour of stale damp from the laundry cupboard that she couldn't get rid of, the soggy smell of vegetables that Pinch had brought in from the garden and left in the sink, and the richness of his tobacco, spilling though from the parlour.

Pinch was waiting in his armchair. He was wearing his gardening waistcoat and his corduroy trousers with the thick leather belt, and his favourite slippers with buckles up to his ankles. He was treating himself to Black Bull's Dung (which he rarely smoked indoors because the strong smell lasted for days). The little book of The Country Parson rested on arm of the chair. Pinch was toying with a thick volume of gardening wisdom but most of his attention was given to his pipe.

To begin with, he made things easy for her by saying nothing. She sat forward on the couch with her hands held tidily in her lap, and prepared to talk with a clear unhurried voice. "Pinch, I have done something very wrong."

He took the pipe from his mouth and let the black-grey smoke, the colour of cannon fire, swirl around his head. "I know all about it. Sergeant Haynes was pleased to report the matter by telephone."

"Yes, yes," she conceded moderately. "There is the episode of the dead mouse down Mrs Hornsby's neck, but I need to tell you something else."

"It is the question of the dead mouse that we need to settle, Peggy."

"Yes, but ..."

"I can't think that there is anything more."

"There is, Pinch."

"There is not, Peggy," he affirmed and placed the pipe between his lips.

She allowed a few moments quiet, then persisted, "Mollie Sweatman ..."

"Mollie Sweatman is a gossip and will make sure that the whole village hears of your bad behaviour."

119

"Yes, and …"

"The mouse. That is what you came to speak to me about."

"Yes," she said, relenting. "I can offer no excuse and I am, truly, ashamed of myself."

"Then I think you should prepare five hundred lines." Something in his face told her not to speak. He leaned forward to collect his matches from the hearth, then took some time refreshing the pipe's burn. "You and I will not talk off it again."

The Silent Six Special was the talk of Doctors throughout the district, so Doctor Johnny made sure that he looked it over before mounting his motorcycle with sidecar and, with a wave of his gauntleted hand, wished Dawes good luck for the rest of the day. It was four o'clock and Dawes wandered about The Street for a quarter of an hour; he wanted to test his list's reaction to the widow's death. It wasn't his fault that he had been in town when the woman's time came. But people might be less forgiving that Dr Johnny, not Dawes, had been there to catch the Willowby child in time. (And, if it wasn't in time, more blame would fall on Dawes.)

But the village seemed strangely peaceful. Although the Post Office was still closed and the Police House was locked, people were quietly getting on with things. Except for the children, of course; they would all be kept indoors. Then he saw that the Becker lad had taken on the job of mending Mr Willowby's bicycle. Untroubled and unhurried, the boy was working through the separate problems with an engineer's curiosity. The Doctor wanted someone to ask what was bothering him, but Pinch and the Vicar were busy with the churchyard's broken fencing, and Farmer Jones wouldn't walk his cattle through the village for another hour. Only Miss Mullens seemed to notice him and she wouldn't be moved. She had spotted something in the large beech tree which she had been observing from the old milestone for all the time that Doctor Dawes had been worrying. Then he heard Jones' horse and cart drawing near from Wretched Lane. Stupidly – and it made him cross – the Doctor feared that it might have been coming to collect the dead.

He hoped that the Constable and the Vicar would complete their business and come walking down The Street. Three heads were better than one. What was Dawes supposed to do? Break into Edie Snag's home when, really, he had no good reason?

He decided to wait for Pinch to return home. He coughed deliberately as he unlatched the policeman's gate and, already having learned that he would get no answer at the front door, dawdled down the garden path. Through the kitchen window, he saw Mrs Pinch writing diligently at their breakfast table. Working behind locked doors. 'She's probably too sad to welcome visitors,' the Doctor surmised, 'or, the Pinches have fallen out.' (Peggy had been occupied for more than forty minutes but had filled less than three sheets with careful, even letters. The alphabet, repeated in perfectly formed capitals with the first stroke of one letter touching the last stroke of the previous. Twenty lines on each page and twenty-five pages to be completed.)

He wanted to knock and ask for her help, but his improper proposal was less than six hours old and she might think that he was pestering.

He returned to The Street and saw that the policeman was alone now, standing at the church gate. When he proceeded down the hill, the Doctor would be able to share some concerns. But Pinch turned away and patrolled not The Street but the mud track of Wretched Lane.

"God," Doctor Dawes sighed irritably. If Pinch got talking to Jones' farmhand, an hour might pass before he'd be seen again.

"Right-ho." He stuck his hands in the pockets of his misshapen sportsjacket and headed for Bulpit Cottage.

No one had seen Edie Snag since the morning service. She hadn't appeared at his lunchtime surgery and she hadn't visited the Post Office, although this was the day when she regularly collected the badly written envelope from a dead neighbour's nephew in Exeter. The Doctor had asked one or two questions; Driver David couldn't recall when he had last seen the old lady and the Vicarage maid had got flustered when the Doctor asked her to think. There was nothing wrong with Bulpit Cottage. The curtains were tidy and the garden path had been swept, but it all seemed too quiet.

He walked through the garden to the back gate where, on his early morning walk, he had noticed young Pepys lurking. He saw the broken hedge where Mollie had hidden the night before and the spent matches which Lovely had dropped when smoking his pipe. Just how many times each day did the cellarman walk to this place?

The Doctor stood on the back path and looked up at the first-floor windows.

"You're worried?" The Red Lion's landlady had forsaken her observation of the beech tree and had followed him.

"I can't find anyone who's seen her since the memorial service, but I don't want to break in."

"There'll be keys," she said, tracing his stare to the windows. "The Post Office, I think, and Miss Carstairs is bound to have one."

"The Post Office is closed," he said, without relaxing his inspection. "I think you could try the old schoolmistress."

"Yes. Yes, I'll get her."

One of Edie's curious habits was to maintain a flowerbed in place of her back doorstep, so that any visitors had to come and go through the front. The back door was reserved for the throwing out of waste tea-leaves, rancid cooking fat and scraps for the birds. When the Doctor tried to peer through windows at the rear of the cottage, he achieved only the darkest shadows of a view. At the side of the house was one window, out of reach, and he had already looked through the front windows earlier in the day (and found nothing wrong).

"Oh Edie, Edie, Edie," he whispered, exasperated, as he walked about her tiny garden. He kicked at some broken orange boxes and wondered if he could make a platform of them over the obstacles of flowerbeds. Then he saw the wheelbarrow.

He pushed it into place, carefully climbed inside and leaned forward until he could rub the glass pane with his coloured handkerchief. The grey shape of Edie Snag's body had collapsed in the corner of the kitchen. One hand reached out as if she had been trying to pull herself through the open door to her parlour.

The Doctor rubbed harder and pressed his face to the glass. He was on the point of falling forward when Queen O'Scots squawked loudly and leapt from the broken orange boxes. He shouted, grabbed for the vine that dressed most of Edie's cottage walls, then went down on one knee and his face smacked on the glass. It didn't break but it hurt. He had to warble like a prep school infant to stop himself from crying. Worse, he had gashed the knee on the barrow's rim and the blood was soaking through his trousers. "Blessed woman," he complained. Then, as the Doctor tried to get his eyes to focus, the grey shape grew more hideous. "Good God," he croaked, his voice uncertain and shaking. A carving knife had been stuck in the back of her neck.

Miss Carstairs arrived, the key already in her hand.

"Don't look inside," he commanded, bending to all fours, then stepping backwards out of the barrow which upturned at the last moment. "Here, give me that!" he said crossly as he put himself right. "Run for PC Pinch. Tell him there's a bad business at Bulpit Cottage."

Edie Snag had always been tiny and poor. In death, she became pitiful. She had fallen awkwardly and, because none of her clothes fitted, they had twisted around her limbs and kept them from lying peacefully. With crooked limbs, screwed up sleeves and skirts and a snapped neck, she looked like a little woman in knots. The wound had bled freely – flowingly, was the word that preyed on Dawes' mind – reaching out in crimson fingers across the bare timber floorboards. The Doctor knelt at her side and laid two fingers against the vertebrae; that made his hand tacky with blood and he was wiping it on a rag when Pinch stepped into the house.

"My God, Pinch, what have we got that keeps doing this?" 'What' instead of 'who' made the murderer especially monstrous.

Pinch laid a gloved hand on the man's shoulder. "Doctor, what can you tell me?"

Ten minutes later, before the detectives arrived from town, Dawes was sitting on the bottom step of the staircase and Pinch was leaning on the banister post. "We have two murders, Pinch, and they centre on Bulpit Cottage." The Doctor was talking with his head in his hands. "The boy from the newspaper, he's always been interested in the place – I saw him outside this morning – and Mollie

123

Sweatman was hiding in the garden hedge last night."

"But Cedar Wells had nothing to do with Edie's home," said Pinch.

"Could the stone that killed Cedar have been thrown from here?"

Pinch shook his head. "Not at all possible," he decided. "But I don't think it could have been thrown from Old School Cottage either. The injuries were at the back of Cedar's head, you see. Mrs Pinch and I remarked at tea time, the windows are all wrong."

The Doctor looked up at him. "There's something more, Pinch. The catapult is missing from my desk."

CHAPTER TWELVE

A Conversation with Dorothy

Things were different this time. Pinch, his Superintendent and the two detectives filled Peggy's parlour. They were sympathetic. They waited patiently while she made a pot of tea, but they didn't expect her to stay in the house; two murders in one week were more than a village policeman's wife should be expected to bear.

Pinch was sitting in his armchair, his knees apart, his tie loose and his collar stud unclipped, an unprecedented licence while on duty in the presence of a superior officer. Peggy noticed the bloodshot strain in his eyes. It was as if they both knew that the murders were drawing closer to home.

Before she left, the couple managed to share whispers:

"Does this evening's play go ahead?"

"It has to," said Pinch. But he had no intention of telling the others about his plan for the Professor's Lodge.

Peggy wanted to smoke, but she knew that Pinch would flinch at his wife showing such independence while his superiors were in the house. She collected her packet of Black Cats and a box of matches from the cutlery drawer and went to the back step. Then she walked up the path and, having no idea where she was going, into The Street. It was empty except for the horse and cart waiting outside Bulpit Cottage. Jones, hoping for an early commission to ferry the corpse to the town's mortuary, was drinking beer in the Red Lion with Seth Lovely. Someone had left freshly cut flowers at the War Memorial and a parcel of library books had been left at Edie's front door. As Peggy progressed up the hill, she kept a look out for

Queen O'Scots; it was unusual for the cat not to have found a strategic position at a time like this. The Postmistress was trying to play the church organ but couldn't decide on an appropriate hymn; each attempt withered away after a few bars or one verse. Peggy heard John Terras working on the blind side of the church roof.

She realised that Pinch had picked up some important clues about the murders – the inconsistencies that made no sense – but he hadn't seen the thread of what was going on.

Peggy knew that she must keep her thoughts to herself. She needed to ask questions but, if she spoke up, she would be either dismissed as silly or in trouble for being truculent. Worse, once started, her mouth might run away with itself, and she'd tell these men just what she thought of them. An outpouring that would do no good. Widow Jenner had died horribly, poor Edie had been murdered, yet the Doctor thought it was all right to press his improper proposal, the Professor wanted to protect their game of peek-a-boo and Pinch was determined to deliver that evening's conspiracy in The Lodge.

"Mother's gone!" squealed a high-pitched voice.

Dorothy Becker ran forward from a hedgerow, panting, fretting and desperate not to cry. The mud on one knee suggested that she had been hiding.

"Now, Dorothy Becker, stand still with your hands by your sides. Your mother can't be far, you know that. She's probably at the back door of the Post Office. You know that the front is shut up."

The young citizen stood, one sock up and one sock down, her dress disordered and her face going this way and that as it tried to cope with a clogged up nose. "Yes, Miss. Because everyone's got keep the murderer out."

"Don't be silly, Dorothy. People need a reason to murder one another, and no one has any reason to harm your Mother or anyone else called Becker."

"But it's different for me. I've heard things and I've told."

"I see." So here was the Vicar's informant, the girl who had overheard Edie Snag's ramblings as she ran through the night, but

126

Peggy realised that she should make nothing of it. Lord, the girl was less than twelve. "Stop crying," she said firmly. "I've always thought of you as a sensible girl."

"And me you, Miss," the girl muttered without a hint of impertinence.

Dorothy Becker looked a poor girl. Just eighteen months before, she had been at death's door. The diphtheria had left her with shallow lungs and white and bony limbs. Miss Carstairs always said that the infection had got to her eyes, but even the schoolma'am's nagging hadn't pushed anyone to do anything about it. Peggy often thought that she could do with a rub.

"Now let me walk you home and we'll wait indoors for Mother."

Peggy collected the girl's cold hand and held it loosely as they made their way up The Street.

"Did you hate boys at school, Miss?"

"I was very quiet, Dorothy. I didn't make friends easily. Yes, boys were difficult, I remember."

"I think, girls are nasty because they're nasty but boys are nasty because they're boys."

Peggy, enjoying the little chat, pretended to think for a moment before nodding. "Yes, I think you're right."

"Our Freddie uses me, dreadfully. I've heard Mother say it." She sighed. She was itching to wipe the back of her hand beneath her runny nose. "He makes me tell things to Father. And, I have to scream out loud so that Mother comes rushing to me while Freddie creeps off." She sighed again, heavily, to emphasise that what was coming was the worst complaint of all. "If we break anything we have to hide it always under my mattress, never his. Does it get better?"

"No, Dorothy. I'm afraid it doesn't."

"I suppose I shall end up hating boys, not every piece of them and not from the bottom of my heart, but still I'll hate them. Oh, am I awful? Should I say that?"

Peggy was nodding. "I call that part of my heart, my anthill. Sometimes it's quiet and still – but it's hard and crusty and never goes away – and when it stirs, it fizzes and festers and works very hard at digging out new pores and stringy bits."

"Yes," said Dorothy. She began to pull the grown-up towards the War Memorial where she wanted them to sit together. She was no longer so anxious about Mother. "Yes, I understand what you're saying, Miss Pinch."

"Mrs Pinch."

"Yes, Miss. Sorry, Miss. Mrs." She frowned; she was sure that she shouldn't call ladies Mrs.

"Mrs when it's Mrs Pinch," explained Peggy. "But Miss when it's on its own."

The girl nodded, her curiosity satisfied. At last, she wiped her nose. Her hand went behind her back, where she wiped it on her dress. (Peggy remembered how, no matter how many times she was told, she was never able to stop doing that as a child.)

Queen O'Scots emerged from the grass verge and walked up the middle of The Street towards the Vicarage. She hoped for some milk, left out by the maid. Dorothy thought that she and Peggy were going to sit on the stone bench of the War Memorial but Peggy led her to the patch of undergrowth behind the structure, hidden from the road. Dorothy was feeling inside the pocket of her dress. Then she remembered that she had sucked the last of the toffees before Miss Edie had been found.

Peggy opened her packet of cigarettes and offered one to the child. "Don't tell," she warned in a friendly tone. Dorothy's moment of hesitation was quickly overtaken by an eagerness to share something naughty with Mrs Pinch.

She took hold of the cigarette and stuck it in the side of her mouth, letting it droop.

"No, no," Peggy said and the girl moved the cigarette to the middle of her lips.

Peggy held out a match. "Don't suck too hard, just gently while it lights."

Peggy waved the match out, dropped it and let the girl watch as Peggy smoked her first couple of puffs. Dorothy copied, and was very proud when she coughed only a little.

"Dorothy, it was Freddie's fault that you trapped yourself in the tree, wasn't it?"

"Mother says I'm not to say because Freddie gets into enough trouble as it is." She mimicked her parent's exasperation: "Oh Lord, Gus, that boy of yours!"

"And the catapult?"

Dorothy nodded, her face almost exploding now from the experience of her first cigarette. "Freddie's."

"And the bruises on Mother's face. They were nothing to do with Father, were they?"

"Of course not! That's why they shout so much. Because they don't hit." Then: "Shall we cook something when we get indoors. Mother wouldn't mind at all and it's fun to do things together."

"Well, I am rather busy, Dorothy. I have to get ready." But Peggy saw the disappointment on the face of her fellow sufferer. "Oh, I'm sure we could bake a cake. I always enjoyed that when I was your age. If not this afternoon, you could come to the Police House one day."

"Do you mean getting ready by cleaning through, or getting ready by putting a different dress on?"

"Well, a better dress, I suppose. I've got to run an errand for Mr Pinch."

"It's always the way. Freddie says I've got to scream and, even though I don't see why I should, I make it the best scream ever. It's the same, isn't it? Me screaming the heavens down, and you putting on your best dress for Mr Pinch's errand."

"I suppose it is."

Dorothy face was a strange yellow-brown greenish colour; she looked sick.

"I managed less than half of my first one," Peggy told her. "You've done very well. Do you want to squeeze it off and save it for later?"

"Better not." Then, more brightly, "I could hide it here, couldn't I? It'd be no trouble, finding time to come back to it."

Peggy found an old recipe pencilled on a scrap of paper. "You must keep it dry." She took the half used cigarette and, sparing a couple of matches, wrapped it in the paper.

Dorothy was already on her knees, preparing the nest. "Shall I tell you what Mother thinks?"

"Do you think you ought?" Peggy cautioned.

The girl, her job completed, stood up from her knees and shrugged. "I don't see why not. It'll make no difference. Mother says it's because we sit down and think about it and decide that it's our fault for not being boys, our fault for not making the boys better and our fault for letting things go wrong. That's why we try so hard in doing what they want us to do. "

"I think Mother could be right," said Peggy.

"I won't ask what you've got to do because Mother says it's always one too many questions that gets me into trouble."

Peggy smiled. "And I won't ask what you've heard and told. But perhaps it would be all right for you to say where you heard these things."

"You know, don't you? Someone's told you."

"Yes, I think they might have done. You heard Miss Snag muttering. 'Miss Carstairs knows all about ...'"

Dorothy finished off, "... and she'll show us all tomorrow."

"When did you hear Miss Snag say that?" They stepped away from the brambles and twigs and sat on the Memorial Bench.

"I was hiding in the hedge when PC Pinch stole muck from Verger Meggastones' garden. I was supposed to be meeting Grace Willowby but she didn't turn up. It's all right, Mrs Pinch, Mother's already smacked me for being out of bed."

"I'm sorry."

"Oh, it's all right. Mother never smacks hard."

"Who else was around?"

"Freddie was upstairs but it was before Father got home."

"No, my love. I mean, when you heard Miss Snag do her muttering."

"Well, she was on her own, but there were others." Her freckled face brimmed with naughty knowledge. "Do you want to know?"

I'm not so sure I do, thought Peggy.

"That Mollie Sweatman was being rumbustious in the grass with Mr Macaulay." Peggy smiled at the girl's tale-telling. She wondered who else in the Willowby household spoke of 'That Mollie Sweatman'.

"Oh! Mrs Pinch! Do you have an imposition?"

Horrified, Peggy realised that she had gathered up her pages of punishment, so that the policemen would not see them, but hadn't found time to hide them in the Welsh dresser before she rushed out. When she had searched her handbag for some paper to wrap the cigarette in, she brought out her lines. The papers were still folded in her free hand.

"Don't be silly. To tell the truth," she said, still working out what she was going to say. "To tell the truth, my handwriting is so bad these days that when I've a few moments, I like to sit and practise."

The little girl beamed. She knew it was a fib but felt, at last, that she and lovely Mrs Pinch were two of the same club. "Well," said Dorothy, wanting to sound understanding, "with poor Miss Snag's death, you would have welcomed a quiet moment to do your skills."

"There's Mother," pointed Peggy. "Coming out of the Post Office, just as I said. Come on, let's hurry to meet her."

"You won't say that Freddie punches Mother, will you?"

"Of course not. We're friends, aren't we?"

"Certainly are!" the girl affirmed proudly as she skipped alongside. "Do you know, I have truly lost count of the lines I've had to do."

"Well," said Peggy, sharing a tip. "I've always found that they're finished sooner if you don't count them in the middle." She beckoned Ruby Becker, then knelt to kiss the child's cold and scruffy cheek. "You mustn't fret, Dorothy, but stay safely in bed tonight."

The child turned and saw the worry on Peggy's face.

"I promise, Miss – and thanks for the, erm, thingy."

CHAPTER THIRTEEN

Night in The Lodge

It was a parlour of apostle teaspoons and china cups, of saucers held decently between lap and chin, and scones and biscuits taken in nibbles so slight that each morsel could be weighed and tested for flavour in the mouth. Miss Carstairs had summoned the Becker wife and the Hornsby woman to Old School Cottage for six o'clock that evening. The Postmistress was there because Miss Carstairs regarded her as one of the most sensible heads in the village. The party had agreed to excuse Peggy: Miss Carstairs and the Postmistress didn't want to embarrass the policeman's wife, and Mrs Hornsby didn't want to be in the same room as 'that woman who knows no better than she ought.' But Peggy wouldn't hear of her being excluded. She sat between the other two and wouldn't budge, even when Miss Carstairs would have welcomed a hand in the kitchen.

"We can't allow the littl'un to be taken off to an asylum," said Ruby Becker, sitting on a hard wood chair, brought forward from the corner of the room.

Miss Carstairs smiled. "I'm sure you mean an orphanage, dear." She explained that she had to reserve the comfortable armchair for herself, because of the knitting-in-progress. It was the commonsense of a housekeeper.

"No, we can't allow it," Mrs Becker repeated.

"The Welfare are much nosier about these matters," said the Postmistress. "It's not like the olden days."

"We've done it before, and not two years ago," argued Mrs

Becker, steadfast and determined. "My Gus will register himself as the father. Who's to say that he isn't? And I do mean an asylum, Miss Carstairs. An asylum."

The room was burdened with unspoken doubts. The Beckers were known to be an unsettled household, not at all like the Willowbys. Gus Becker struggled as a father, and Peggy was the only one present who thought that Dorothy would make a worthy older sister. But, Miss Carstairs regretted, the scarlet fever ruled the Willowbys out. Teaspoons clinked against china, jam was passed around for the scones and Earl Haig looked down from a patriotic print.

"I don't care what you all think," Ruby said. "No one in our parish could be a better mother to this little mite."

Then Mrs Hornsby declared: "I think it's a good idea, Ruby," bringing Peggy to attention. "But you will need help. Young Freddie's such a handful at the moment. I know he'd be happy to spend some afternoons with me."

Peggy realised that Mrs Hornsby understood that helping little Fred was the solution to Gus and Ruby's difficulties. "Yes," she said, "and I'd love to have Dorothy for an hour or two. When you think so, Ruby, of course."

Miss Carstairs was surprised by the turn of the conversation but she read such confidence on Peggy and Hornsby's faces that she fell in with the idea. "Freddie's very fond of cooking, isn't he? I'd look forward to having him in my kitchen. I do so miss showing kiddies what to do, you know."

But the Postmistress fidgeted at the back wall. "Well, I would feel much better if the Vicar's wife were here."

Mrs Becker continued, as if she hadn't heard the interjection. "This village is full of tittle-tattle but we've always been careful to keep our own secrets. This new baby is our ..." She hesitated over the word, and when she said, 'responsibility,' the others sensed that she really meant 'fault'.

The Postmistress remained uncomfortable. "I always feel that someone from the Vicarage gives these arrangements a tolerable authority. Can't we wait for the Rector's wife to get here?"

Ruby looked at Peggy and Mrs Hornsby. "It is agreed, then. Mrs Jenner's baby stays in our cottage?"

"My dear, are you sure you want your Gus to come forward as the father?" asked Miss Carstairs.

Ruby stuck out her chin. "There's no shame in it. No shame at all in a parish caring for its own."

Of course, it was nonsense to imagine that Gus Becker had ever been unfaithful. Well, perhaps a few minds might have entertained the rumour before this evening, but Ruby had stood up for herself so well that none of the women believed her household could be burdened with such skeletons. Gus and Ruby were devoted to their family; and was young Freddie anything worse than a particularly naughty son?

'Nothing here that I can't sort out,' thought Miss Carstairs. And how wonderful that Mrs Hornsby and the policeman's wife were prepared to work together. She sat back in her armchair, the knitting-in-progress pressing against her hip, and she allowed herself a faintly smug smile.

The ladies sipped from the lips of their delicate cups. A couple sighed, another stirred her tea. Ruby checked that a hanky was safely tucked in her sleeve, raised her eyes and looked at the grand clock on Miss Carstairs' wall

"So," the Postmistress sighed, and no one interrupted her. "It begins with me having a word with the deanery midwife, does it?" No one said that she shouldn't.

Pinch had sent the word out. Folk were to stay with their families tonight. Those who lived on their own should sit with their neighbours. For those who didn't want that, the Red Lion could stay open for as long as it was needed.

The Policeman and the Vicar met on the church green at a quarter to nine.

"You're ready for our walk to The Lodge?"

Pinch nodded curtly, brought out a pipe and leaned against the kissing gate as he got it going. "We must give Peggy time to prime the snare," he said.

134

"Do you have to make it sound so ungodly, Pinch?" The Vicar felt the evening drizzle on his cheeks. He pulled his coat collar close.

"The Doctor is out of harm's way?"

"I'm afraid I made him so worried about poor Edie's death that he's gone off to present himself to the Coroner." He added, "I fear I've been unnecessarily cruel to the little man."

"Better that than risk his involvement in our skulduggery. He has to take account of professional discipline."

"Don't we all," said the Reverend. "Don't we all."

"He knew about Cedar's double life but could do nothing for her. He was away from the village when Widow Jenner died, and now he's found the body of his favourite patient. How is he?"

"Oh, I think he'll be able to cope with it, Pinch. As you say, he's a professional man."

"I meant, Vicar, that he might know too much."

"Oh! Yes, I see. Too much for his own good, you mean. My word, Pinch, do you think there'll be more murders?"

Lights were on in the Willowby and Becker homes, and a lamp in the attic suggested that the Postmistress and her brother had agreed to sleep together, just as they used to do when canes tapping on window panes warned that Zeppelins were overhead. Pinch had made it clear to the Hornsbys that there must be no stargazing tonight. He had hinted that devil's work was in hand. For a couple whose reputations thrived on talk of witchcraft and ghouls, they quickly promised that they would be early to bed. Miss Carstairs had agreed to sit with the Vicarage maid. They weren't to be alarmed, said Pinch, if the vagrant Gregory turned up to sit in their kitchen. The Verger's stance would have been a curious one in any other character. He decided that his station was at the rope of the parish bell, so that he could sound the alarm at a moment's notice. He resolved to be there each night until the murderer was caught. The Red Lion looked like the most homely of places with its well provisioned hearth, extra victuals including a hot punch, and the sack of blankets which was traditionally kept for victims of house-fires, floods, fallen trees and snowdrifts. When young Pepys asked who was looking after the Professor, Seth told him that The Lodge was such a convoluted dwelling that a murderer would likely get lost before he found the man in circus spectacles. "Makes no difference," said the boy. "He should be here with the rest of us." Fortunately, no one took up the suggestion and Pinch's plan remained intact.

The Vicar and the policeman had taken charge; it was as if the village had bound together as it crept through the night of danger.

Pinch took his pipe from his mouth. "Our Mollie?"

The rain was light but it was settling in and the grey clouds meant there would be little moonlight tonight.

"She's sleeping at Thurrocks Farm," said the Vicar.

Pinch saw the sense in that. Mollie started work there before six each morning. "A round of the farms wouldn't be amiss." He weighed the pros and cons of asking the Divisional Inspector for support, but the old man would expect Pinch to patrol on his bicycle.

The Vicar read his thoughts. "We must look after ourselves. Dawes should be back before ten. I'll ring him up and ask him to bring the Silent Six into service."

Pinch nodded a thank you. The conversation rested for a minute. Both men watched for any movement in The Street. There was, it seemed, a pleasure in sharing a silence.

"It's the same in my line," Pinch said.

"You mean the professions?"

"All this argument about the RAC men. Should they take over traffic direction? Let them have it, I say. It's the village copper who's likely to be taken away from his duties and assigned to the middle of a road for hours on end. Bring on the RAC boys, I say."

The Vicar nodded and said, "John Terras was more difficult. He says he'll stay at the Lion, but that won't suit a man who always needs a job to do. I put it in Miss Mullens' head that she should suggest keeping Meggastones company, but she can't go as far as telling Terras what to do." After a moment's reflection, both men chuckled at the prospect of the Verger welcoming John's presence through the night.

The church clock struck the three-quarter hour. Pinch stepped forward and surveyed The Street. "Well, now. Do we carry on with our prank?"

"This is no time to withdraw our troops, Pinch. We must press on."

They saw Peggy's grey figure proceeding up the hill. She wore her second-best cloche hat and a thick coat, but she had no umbrella. Pinch wondered if she was walking a little pigeon-toed; she seemed to wobble like a child treading the plank.

"Better she doesn't see us," he said and they withdrew to the shadows of the graveyard.

Peggy had not visited The Lodge before. The fat stodgy house had ruminated for years, congealing like a bulbous frog with digestive problems, on the posh side of the village where residences stood back from the road and were protected by yew hedges so that passers-by could only see the top storey windows. Few people had reason to walk down Back Lane (pronounced 'Bach', if you lived there). She had chosen a roundabout route.

She pretended that she was on a twilight stroll. She waved a gloved hand at the Vicarage, though she saw no one there to greet, and when she walked along Wretched Lane she paused to look over the vale of farmland. Then she wandered along the broad ditch, called the Sunken Road though it had never been a proper way. Multitudes of blackberries had grown here before the War. It brought her to the back of The Lodge. She struggled to push the old gate open. The Professor did not spend time in his garden and, as Peggy trod up the muddy path, it looked a dirty, dingy home.

She found her first evidence before she reached the door. The missing catapult had been left, half hidden, in the last bed of weeds. Left, deliberately for Peggy to find? She stooped, gathering the hem of her coat close to her knees. Peggy felt cold. She realised that the Professor was treating her visit as a game. The most important game of his life, perhaps, and he had wagered high stakes. She touched the exhibit, moving it half an inch, but she left it on the ground. After all, the game was murder and an important piece of the puzzle should be left for Pinch's advice.

The Professor had insisted that she should walk in without knocking but it was still a difficult thing to do. This wasn't Miss Carstairs' Cottage or the Vicarage where she might be able to explain wandering in unannounced. But this evening she was playing burglars, so she gripped the hooked iron handle and pushed.

In the small square lobby she met the first of the drapes that hung at every turn in this house. They hid doorways, sheltered shelves, concealed alcoves; they kept the daylight away and, if they worked against the draughts, they also kept the dust of years. These weren't everyday curtains but heavy lengths of woven or stitched tapestry, some so old that they were faded and threadbare.

It would have been so easy to shout 'Hello' or 'Anyone home?' But Peggy played the game. Without a word, she walked through the next door.

The Lodge was silent. No clocks ticked. No floorboards groaned. Where was he?

She had promised that he could peep at her as she walked about his home and she had always known that he would be clever at it. But this good?

Then she realised that he would have thought of nothing else for twenty-four hours. He would have planned every moment. He would have bored Judas holes into walls, constructed priest holes and secret passages where she could not see them. He had a criminal mind, Pinch had often said, and he would get away with any crime he committed.

Now she was viewing his smoking room. In Peggy's modest Police House, she would have called it her parlour. The only armchair rested in the far corner, where a row of wooden tobacco barrels stood on the mantelpiece. A naughty drawing hung in an elaborate frame above them and, as Peggy went closer, she felt the Professor's eyes on the back of her neck. She leaned forward to stroke a fingernail on the glass, along the line of the plump woman's thigh. Her curiosity, with its tickly excitement, turned her tummy queasy. Horrible, that a man could sit alone in this room with an obscene picture so prominently displayed. Somewhere, he was watching, enjoying the prudishness in her puddle of confusion.

Somewhere, he would be imagining her. Her, on the wall.

She stepped back into the middle of the room. She had been here for twenty minutes, no longer, and it was probably black outside but the drapes allowed her no way of seeing.

Of course, the drapes were here to help exclude all time from the house. There wasn't a clock in the place. She felt uncomfortably warm. She took off her hat and gloves and laid them on an arm of the chair. She pushed a drape aside, opened a door and walked across the bottom of the staircase to the next room, a narrow library that ran the length of the house. Bookcases were screwed to each wall, a turmoil of rugs overlapped each other on the floor. The furniture was ornate, but in a dowdy way. She thought that much of the woodwork had been lacquered with blacks or smoky greys. The clawed feet of the table legs, the chair back that looked as if it was a face gone wrong and the bare cherubs on picture frames could each have been frozen in a moment and coated in barren colours so that they would never move again.

Three black tables were stationed, like ugly stepping stones, in the middle. Two had inclined tops, one with maps, the other held a heavy leather bound book open at its middle pages. The third table was for sitting at. She turned around and was ready to leave the room when she noticed a wall mirror, taken down and propped on the floor. Peggy understood at once. He had placed it so that, from some hiding place, he could see the backs of her calves as she stepped past. She had spoilt it for him by closing the library door on him. She realised that, for the Professor, the game was already in full flow. Why didn't she nudge the mirror so that it lost its focus?

She left the library and moved to climb the staircase but when she reached for the handrail, her fingers shot back – as if they had been burned or shocked. One hand rubbed the other, and she stared at the boss moulded on the base of the black timber banister. It was a feral cat's head, grinning hideously with two pointed teeth and eyes that had been dug out.

"Nonsense," she whispered. As she stepped on the stairs, she told herself that she wasn't playing the game properly. Rather than being jumpy at every turn, she should be teasing him to come out of hiding. Like an actress on the stage. Except, Peggy had never seen an actress on a stage. She unbuttoned her coat, slipped it from her shoulder and, as it trailed behind her, she held onto the collar until the last moment, so that it fell as the first discarded layer of her clothing. She didn't turn around, but she was sure that the Professor's round face had emerged from the dimness to watch her ascent to the first floor. This was one moment when she was sure where he was. He would be behind and below her, trying to glimpse up her skirt and hoping to see the bare backs of her knees. She climbed, higher and higher, and she sensed his eyes relish her rear view.

Peggy began to get the creeps. She felt her bottom muscles twitch; the inside line of her legs felt peculiarly undressed.

The house spoke again and Peggy felt worse. The shift of a timber floor, sending creaks across adjacent ceilings and making pipes weigh against their brackets, was no accident. The Professor knew where to press a footprint that would bring Peggy to attention. She knew that he knew, and the Professor knew that too, and so his trick carried more than a tinge of sadism.

When she reached the stairhead, she gave in to her nerves. She spun round, ready to catch him red-faced and awkward. But no man was there.

She thought, 'I want Pinch to come. I want Pinch to knock on the door and draw the unsavoury Professor away.'

Upstairs, the arrangement of rooms was so small and cramped that she was sure she had found only half the first floor. The Lodge must have a second staircase. This, in a house which had already made her think of priest holes and secret passages.

Where was he?

Something was wrong. She knew that the Professor would be peeking at her – from the edges of thick curtains or the corners of grimy window panes – but he had been wanting to steal her image for so many years that she was sure he would keep in bounds. No, this was a different unease. Her sixth sense told her that she was being spied on for a trick. Someone else was in The Lodge. A chill caught the back of her neck and she twisted round to look for curtains billowing at an open window. But there was nothing. Every old house, like this one, had cold corners that made people think of ghosts and burglars, but these spirits were no more than nooks that never drew in the warmth. That's what she told herself.

Peggy's dress and blouse were enough to keep her warm on a cold night, but each time her arm reached for a handle or a ledge, the dwelling's air seemed to chill the moisture in her armpits and the small of her back. Downstairs a door creaked like a bird in pain, and she heard a heavy thud as if something had been trodden on. She knew that she wasn't alone in the house with the Professor; there was another intruder.

Quickly, she poked her head into each of the three available rooms. When she found a bedroom, she looked under the bed. When she saw a wardrobe, she opened the door and looked in the bottom. As she worked, more and more quickly, – first in one room, then in another, then back to the first – she felt her attitude change. She was no longer hunting down a spy. She was looking for a body.

Again, she remembered Pinch's consideration of the murders. The Professor was in the middle of it all, taking no part but always there. At the elm tree when Dorothy was stuck, in the graveyard at night, on The Street when Cedar was killed, and the first to knock on the door when poor Edie's body had been found. The murderer might rest easy if the unreliable, unpredictable Professor was removed from the picture.

Her imagination gathered pace. If the Professor's body was suspended behind one of the drapes or cramped in one of the hidden cupboards, the shifting floorboards and the eyes on the back of her neck must have come from someone else – the murderer still in the house.

From the outside, The Lodge had looked hideous and built to keep secrets. The ground floor had been altered with large rooms that suited the man who lived in them but, upstairs, the Professor's home made no sense. Rooms were set at awkward angles, linked by passages that might once have been rooms themselves. It was as if two homes had been knocked into one and not all the spaces could be put to good use. Peggy was stepping through one of these odd dog-legs when she looked out of the window and saw that she was crossing the roof of the back porch.

When she turned back to the room —

"Ugh!" Her hand went to her throat and bile spilled into her mouth.

Mollie Sweatman's face had startled her. Not the girl herself but a quarto-sized drawing of her, framed behind glass and hung on the wall. She was bare. The lines were incomplete and the shading no more than hints, but he had caught the weary bitterness in her eyes and the doleful, over-fed look of her cheeks. He had stripped her not only of her clothes but also her brash wilfulness. Here, Mollie had the face of a woman who thought little of herself and resented that others were better. She didn't sit easily. Something was aching, an ankle or elbow or a muscle in her back; she was a woman who wanted to leave.

Peggy stood, fascinated. Mollie's breasts looked so real, so … puffy, and her stomach hung a little over her lap, hiding her womanhood and making her look motherly. But her throat was wrong. Was it crooked? Or cricked? "Cock-eyed," Peggy said quietly and reached forward to straighten the frame.

"Ah!"

She stepped back and brought all her fingers to hide her face. As the frame moved from side to side on its thread, Mollie neck was at the fulcrum of the movement. It looked as if she was being hung on a gallows.

Peggy wanted to run from the room, but her waters told her not to turn back. Go forward.

Feeling more and more like Alice Through the Looking Glass, she stooped to walk through a door, which should have been a cupboard door, and she stepped into a square passage that should have led to another room, but had a dead end.

It had no carpet, no windows and no way out, except for the little play-door behind her, yet the narrow fireplace, unused for years, suggested that this hiding place had once been lived in. The only furniture was a heavy oak chest, bound in irons, that sat in the middle of the room. Peggy walked around it, touching the corners, leaning over to look down on it. An emblem had been carved naively on the face. She knelt down to trace the design; it was, she decided, two misshapen letters. ƕ.ɼ. She winced as her weight pressed a nailhead into her knee. "King Henry," she said, quietly but excitedly, as she shifted an inch or two. The chest was hundreds of years old.

Trying the lid and testing the heavy locks, she recalled a history that had been promoted during her childhood, when a stout and whiskery high Anglican had been her parish priest. He told the Sunday school how eighteenth century peasants in the neighbouring village had risen up against their incumbent and destroyed much of the church property. Two villains had been hung and an old woman had been cast out of the community (their fate held up as a lesson for all). The parish chest had been ripped from its moorings during the riot and, though it had never been recovered, many people said that it had been buried on the farmlands between that parish and Peggy's village. She remembered how her contemporaries, unable to make sense of the word 'incumbent', had turned this history into games of St Cumbant's Treasure. Now, Peggy was kneeling at an old parish chest, discoloured by years of being half sunken in the earth. The Professor, or a previous occupant of The Lodge, had found St Cumbant's Treasure and installed it in this little back room.

She couldn't budge the lid. Her frustrated groans were interrupted by creaking floorboards, softly trodden footsteps and the moan of old timbers as someone shifted their weight from one foot to another. She expected to Professor to catch her at any moment. She was sure that someone else was in the room, but every time she turned around, she found that she was alone in a room without windows or hiding places.

"Oh, God, let Pinch come soon," she whispered hoarsely.

The clang of the front door bell, like a hollow bidding before an unholy mansion, answered her prayer. At last, the Vicar and Pinch had arrived, and they summoned the Professor so insistently that he could be in no doubt that they intended to ring and knock until he answered. She heard him move from the library to the lobby; he had been downstairs all the time. Then the Vicar and the policeman were introducing themselves, ushering the Professor into his study and securing a position that would keep him occupied for as long as they needed.

Their arrival seemed to emphasise Peggy's responsibility in their scheme and she set to with fresh gusto, rapping on the joints of the stubbornly locked chest. "Bloody," she spat mutedly. "Bloody, bloody," and then with an extra effort, "Bloody!"

A split dowel shot from one of the wooden hinges. Peggy had sprung a secret lock.

At first, she thought that the cabinet was being used as a linen box, but the musty smell told her that none of the cloth had been laundered or aired. Certainly, none had been pressed. As she leafed through the pale colours, more often the off-whites of cheap clothing, she realised that she had found the Professor's booty from the washing lines and laundry baskets of the village. Here was his collection of ladies' undergarments. More specifically, their knickers.

The find, which should have turned her stomach, amused her. (Peggy had no notion of how a gentleman bachelor might use a woman's necessaries.) As she burrowed down, finding pants of different sizes, some stretched through years of wear, some marked with stains that wouldn't wash out, some with stains that were too strident for words, Peggy fancied a prospect of matching each item to its familiar seat. "Oh, what stories," she laughed. "More than a hundred. More than two hundred! He must have been pinching our pants for years."

Peggy wanted to giggle. Stretched and misshapen ones for Postmistress Mary. Grey and long-legged ones for the Hornsby woman. Here's one for the Vicar's maid, scrubbed thin. And a soft, hardly worn pair that would have suited Mrs Willowby's bottom. Peggy bit her bottom lip; this could be too much fun.

She remembered just two or three rumours. Last Easter, the Postmistress had accused Freddie Becker of stealing from her washtub, but he had been able to account, wide-eyed and bewildered, for every minute of his day. Then Miss Carstairs had mentioned that 'a solitary snowdrop' had disappeared from her line but she had been content to blame the squirrels or magpies, for decency's sake. Peggy had no doubt, all her own smalls were in their right place and she wouldn't find anything of hers in the Professor's cache. That, she daydreamed, was a little disappointing.

Downstairs, the Professor was entertaining his guests in a bid to avert any revelation that the Constable's wife was upstairs. Peggy could hear him agreeing with everything the Vicar said and emphasising the policeman's contribution to the parish. He sounded like a wretched little man.

When she began to draw from the bottom of the chest, she brought out a parcel of letters daintily tied with blue ribbon. She sat back on her heels and read a paragraph from every third or fourth leaf. She knew at once that these had not been written in the Professor's careful copperplate hand but, of course, these were letters that he had received rather than sent. They were love letters, written from the woman in Bulpit Cottage. Not Edie Snag, but poor Tilly Lovely who had fled the village to keep her pregnancy quiet. She hoped the child would be called Henry, although, she feared, he would have to put up with being called Pepys because of her choice of a new name. In another, she asked to meet her lover behind her Bulpit Cottage. Peggy wanted to return the letters to their hiding place – she felt sympathy for the Professor in his lonely home, with his curious hobby and his broken heart – but the letters were important evidence about the murders of Edie Snag and Cedar Wells. She retied them, making a neat bow with the ribbon, and placed them at her feet.

She had already found two secrets in the chest; she was sure that if the Professor had the old parish covenant, she would find it amongst the trophies of purloined smalls. She went further and more thoroughly, leaning forward until she was almost in the chest herself. Again, she felt a pair of eyes on her. She reached behind to make sure that her dress was smoothly covering her bottom and thighs.

Voices at the bottom of the stairs. The Professor was recalling how Pinch loved trains, and wasn't the Reverend famous for his motoring adventures? He was sure that they would be interested in his collection of technical drawings; he had found them in a Parisian curio shop. The French had always been good with engines, he'd heard.

"Soup!" said Pinch.

'Soup?' Peggy wondered, her head in the wooden box.

"Soup?"

She heard the suspicion in the Professor's voice. He was beginning to wonder why these two authority figures had called on him on a dark and dreary night. Then, "Punch!" he announced with a juvenile pitch to his voice. "Night-comers to The Lodge won't drink soup. Not soup. Hot punch. Come this way, gentlemen." The Professor's idea was to distract his visitors from climbing the stairs but it fell in with the conspirators' plan. Warming punch on his range and sharing it convivially at his hearth would occupy him for thirty minutes or more.

Peggy got to work but she was sure that someone was watching her. She sat on her heels again and looked around. Really, there was nowhere for an interloper to hide. She was laying the knickers smooth and flat in the chest when she sensed that something in the bottom was causing unevenness. As soon as her fingertips went to the base, she felt the package taped to a corner of the wooden frame. This time, there was no doubting what she had found. The parish documents were wrapped in a leather roll, small enough to fit in a lady's handbag, if not her purse. Peggy checked that the parchment was marked with old fashioned handwriting, then hurried to the top of the stairs.

Pinch, hearing her footsteps, appeared at the bottom and motioned that she should throw the parcel to him, without a word. He caught it, and a second signal said that she was to go straight home.

But Peggy had one last job to do. She returned to the little bare room and completed her laying out of the Professor's trophies. But she wanted to leave something behind to show that, although she had rifled through the stock, she thought none the worse of him. A handkerchief, she decided, would be a suitable token. She reached inside her dress and produced a plain, everyday hanky. She folded into quarters and tucked it between the layers of cotton. She hoped that he would find it – in days, weeks or months to come – and see it as her little trick on him. Then, as she was rubbing a linen gusset between a thumb and finger and wondering if she dared hold a stranger's underwear close to her face, she was caught in the act by a shrill voice.

"It's mine!"

CHAPTER FOURTEEN

Wise Counsel

Peggy spun so sharply that she landed on her bottom with her arms outstretched. The Becker girl was standing in the middle of the bare room.

"Dorothy! What are you doing here?"

"Same as you," shrugged the girl. "We're looking for that catapult, ain't we? I've found it in the garden and it's mine."

"I can't let you have it yet. Constable Pinch needs it."

"It's mine," Dorothy repeated with a touch of sulk.

"What made you think it was here?"

"The Professor's gone mental. He's forever having interests in things which-art mine."

Peggy smiled. She was always picking up the lass's interpretation of the Lord's Prayer's text in her everyday speech.

"Old Dawes ain't got it and I ain't got it, so the Professor's got to be next, ain't he?"

"Ain't isn't nice, Dorothy. Try to say hasn't."

Immediately, the girl thought of three or four examples where changing ain't to hasn't wouldn't do. Next thing, Miss Peggy would be saying how her parents are worrying and she shouldn't be out so late.

Peggy had recovered herself. She closed the chest of underwear, then picked up the bundle of love letters. She brushed herself down, lightly. "My dear, I've got to take these things down to Constable Pinch so that he can speak with the Professor. He'll want me to keep out of the way, so I'll be able to walk you home."

"Don't take them!" the girl said urgently. "I don't want you to. I don't want anyone to speak to the Professor."

"But, dear, can't you see that Mr Pinch will want to ask questions?"

"Then take them home with you. Mr Pinch can see them in the Police House, can't he? Wait till then, can't he?"

"Yes," relented Peggy. "I suppose he can. Come now, we need to walk you home. You shouldn't be out this late."

Dorothy waited.

Peggy patted the sides of her hair. "They'll be worrying," she said.

Dorothy sighed.

They walked together up Back Lane, the high hedgerows protecting them from enquiring faces at the posh windows. "Constable Pinch laid down very strict rules for tonight," Peggy said, trying to sound stern. "No one was to be out of doors unless it was very necessary."

But she couldn't have been very good at being strict, because her young friend only smiled and held her hand more surely. "I know. Mother made us cross our hearts. That's why I can't let you take me all the way home. Mrs Pinch, we are true friends and I will always do just as you want, but you do see, don't you? I've got to sneak in on my own tonight."

Peggy remembered how, as a child, being brought home was a fate more dreadful than most others. "We'll go the back way to your garden and I'll leave you at the gate."

"Oh, thank you, Miss."

"But I will be watching to make sure that you go straight in."

"I will. I promise, I will." Dorothy had gathered pace and Peggy felt her wanting to skip.

Peggy wanted to be quick too. The night was black in this hidden part of the village. She looked forward to reaching the more familiar ground of The Street with its little grass alleys.

"Is it awfully dangerous being out tonight?" Dorothy asked.

"We all want to catch the man who murdered poor Edie and Miss Wells. As we get closer to him, he's bound to get desperate. Who knows what he'll do?"

149

Dorothy nodded thoughtfully. "You're very clever, Mrs Pinch."

"Oh, I don't think so."

"No, you are. You always talk about the man who murdered us. Always, 'he' did and 'his' what's it. Just so that no girl will ever think that you suspect her."

"My! You're the clever one, Dorothy Becker. I think we've all underestimated you."

"Well, a girl does a lot of listening when she's sick in bed for weeks. Especially, if people in the room think she's too weak to make sense of what they say."

"My goodness."

"But you do know who the murderer is, don't you?"

"Yes, Dorothy. I think I've been sure of it for two days but we've got to be careful."

"Careful not to warn him?"

"Yes."

"Or her?"

"Oh, I'm not saying."

"And, I suppose, careful not to tell the men too early in case they make a mess of things."

"Well, yes, that is something to be wary of."

As they reached the church green and turned down the Waddie that ran behind the cottages, Peggy noticed that lights were still on at the Red Lion. She saw shapes moving around the Vicarage kitchen and the dim lantern burned in the Post Office attic. It had passed midnight but folk were too nervy to go to their beds.

"You do believe in us girls doing things, don't you?" asked Dorothy.

Peggy didn't correct 'us girls'. She remembered how irritating Miss Carstairs' rules of grammar used to be when young Peggy was trying to have a grown-up conversation with her. She said, "Life is teaching me that. 'Us girls doing things.' Yes, I'm believing in it more and more. But a woman must always be mindful of the promises that she has made to her husband, Dorothy. Promises made before God are just the same as promises made to God."

Dorothy understood. She quietly said, "Our vows," nodding.

"Our vows, Dorothy. The most important promises a girl can make. You'll remember that for me, will you?"

"Oh, me? No, I'm not getting married. You won't catch me with a baby either."

"Dorothy! How can you say such a thing! Just think how disappointed your mother would be, and don't you want me to be proud of you when I see you walking up The Street with your first pram." Then she made light of it. "But you're far too young to make up your mind about such things."

"You've not done it," she said reasonably.

"That's because I've not been blessed yet, Dorothy. God takes his time, sometimes, that's all."

"I suppose you'll tell me that Miss Carstairs has filled herself up with other people's children."

Peggy was puzzled, but came up with the answer. "You mean fulfilled herself."

"'cept sometimes," Dorothy ventured, "when you are talking to Miss Carstairs, well, it sometimes feels that she has had a child. Do you know what I mean, you get a sort of comfortable feeling about her, don't you? Do you think, God took away the Vicar's little boy as a punishment?"

"A test, maybe. No more than a test."

Peggy wanted to be quiet for a few moments but the girl's ideas were coming in a rush.

"So, a man needn't get married but a girl should do. Things being normal, that is."

Yes, thought Peggy. And that's why the world is never fair to us.

Dorothy was wanting to skip again. "What I want to know is, what was she doing there?"

"Now, you'll have to tell me who and where," Peggy joked.

"That Mollie Sweatman. She was hiding in The Lodge while you were doing your scurrying. It made me laugh. The Professor was supposed to be at home on his own. First, you turn up. Then I creep in after you. Then, before we know it, that Mollie Sweatman's dodging in and out."

"Where did you see her, Dorothy?"

"Well, for one, she was hiding in the room next to yours."

"She couldn't have been. I looked around and no one was there and there was nowhere to hide."

"Behind the drapes! Didn't you see her toes? I did. I poked my head through that tiny door and caught them wriggling above the skirting. But what was she doing there?"

"I think," said Peggy, "that she was after her own secrets, Dorothy."

"That Mollie. More to her than meets your eyes, Mother says. Yes, it makes sense. The Professor had my catapult and I came to get it back. He also had something off that Mollie Sweatman and she came to get it back. Certainly makes you think, don't it?"

"Doesn't it," Peggy corrected.

"Definitely do," said Dorothy, and Peggy left the grammar alone because it was a favourite phrase of Mr Becker. "Do you know what she was after?"

"No, Dorothy, dear. I'm afraid to say that I don't, but it is one of those important questions that I need to answer before very much longer. If I don't, well, who knows how things could go wrong."

"Gosh, you mean that Mollie Sweatman could be done in!" But then a more important matter dawned on the little girl. "We're getting near. I suppose I ought to be thinking up a good story, just in case I'm caught." Queen O'Scots was sitting on the Becker gatepost, her black shape no more than a shadow against the thick hedgerow.

"Oh, I think the truth would stand you in good stead."

"Yes, but, well, comes a time when a girl has to do much better than the truth. The truth is very lame when you've been adventuring. Freddie always looks to me for our excuses. He says my stories are better than any he's heard about in books." She adopted a low gruff tone. "That girl's storytelling will be our downfall, Ruby Becker."

Peggy smiled.

"That's what Father says," explained Dorothy.

"Yes, I guessed as much from your voice."

Mrs Becker was standing on her back porch. Feet astride, arms folded, and the firmest set of her chin.

"Oh Cripes, I'm for it. Look at her standing like she is. Oh Lor, I suppose it's too late to pray."

"It's never too late, Dorothy, but you have been disobedient on the very night when you should have been well behaved."

Mother began to tap one of her slippered feet. Fingers of one hand lay restlessly on the other forearm.

"Oh, Cripes."

"Would you like me to come with you? I could explain what a help you've been to me."

Dorothy Becker bit her bottom lip. "No, Aunt Peggy. Thank you very much, but no. No, there are some things that a girl has to face on her own."

The night crept on. The shadows, with no prospect of reaching forward for daylight, sank into the dull shapes of the houses and trees and any sounds of life were stifled by a blanket of damp weather. Leaves and grass, having taken all the drizzle they could bear, dipped their tips and let go of the fresh moisture and the village wildlife burrowed an inch or two deeper into the banks and verges. The Postmistress and her brother dozed in the light of their lanterns while old Gregory, the tramp who always passed through the neighbourhood at this time of year, slept soundly in a shed behind the Red Lion. At half past one, the Vicar walked the retired schoolmistress home and stayed outside until her bedroom light went out.

By two, only Lovely and Pepys were awake in the inn. Seph had sent the landlady to bed and was locking up when Pepys, in a borrowed dressing gown, arrived at the foot of the stairs.

When neither man spoke, Seph knew what the lad had come down to say.

Pepys took Verger Meggastone's chair at the smouldering hearth and waited for the cellarman to join him with two ales. Their faces were tired and colourless and their voices so soft that their heads came together as they listened.

"You've taken a special interest in me," the lad said, his chin down, his eyes concentrating as he tried to put the pieces of the jigsaw together. "Last night, when you caught me looking at Bulpit Cottage, you weren't really bothered about what I was up to. You wanted me to talk. You didn't care if I talked about anything or nothing; seems to me, you were getting to know me."

Seth stirred in his seat. He felt the tears come to his eyes.

"Then there's Mr Hardcastle at the paper. Always been good to me, Mr Hardcastle, so there's another old man who takes an interest in me. From the start, I couldn't make out why he sent me here. He said he wanted me to investigate the murder but he knew young Pepys couldn't do that. It seems to me, he sent me here to find out the truth, all right, but not the truth of the murder. The truth about something else."

He was handling the empty pipe, the present from Seth, rubbing the bowl into the palm of one hand, then twisting the stem. "Now, you say that your daughter used to live in Bulpit Cottage, and the Professor tells me that she had to leave the village. He doesn't say because she was having a baby, but sure enough, that's what he wants me to think. I'd think nothing of that, except for this photo." He stretched back so that he could reach into the folds of his dressing gown. He fingered a small postcard with serrated edges and creased corners. He had no need to pass it to old man. "I found it beneath the moth sheet in Mother's chest. It's a picture of Bulpit Cottage. Now, what's my Ma'am doing with a picture like that? You're my grandfather, Mr Lovely, and it seems to me only right that you tell me so."

Seth replied quickly. "I don't know who your father is, lad. I didn't know at the time and your mother's not spoken to me since she left. She was old enough to look after herself and, well, Mr Hardcastle was there, taking an interest."

Pepys lifted his eyes for the first time. "You think …"

"I said I don't know," Seth repeated sharply. Then, recovering his patience, he said. "The pipe belonged to your Uncle Richard. I'll tell you about him one day, but not yet."

"The Professor …"

"Oh, God's Sake, son, stop listening to what the Professor tells you!"

"He says that Constable Pinch has too much to do with these matters. He says, Pinch didn't take up his position in the village until years later, but now and again he was here."

Seth stuck his boot on the fire, pushing the burnt logs to the back. "I said I don't know."

"You see, I think Mr Pinch gets things right. I think he knows all about this village and the people in it, and when Mistress Wells got hit by that rock, I think Mr Pinch got it right then. That's why Mr Hardcastle knew it was safe to send me here; he knew there was no murderer left in the village. He knew it was safe for me to poke my nose in and ask questions. He knew that it was important for me to find out the truth because, before long, it would be too late."

At three in the morning, Pinch in his slippers and pyjamas bottoms brought two cups of tea upstairs and, having asked "Are you all right?" sat on the edge of their bed with his back to his wife. "I'm sorry."

That was part of the trouble. She didn't want him to be sorry. Neither did she want his lovemaking to be dripped with 'Does it hurt?' 'Am I too heavy?' or 'There, there.' 'Nearly finished' was worst of all; it made him sound like a child on the lavatory.

Pinch was drunk on the Professor's punch; without that, he would not have risked the intimacy. She was worried that he had taken her without care – that was so unlike him – but Peggy felt soiled rather than pregnant. She rolled over so that he wouldn't see her disappointment.

The problem is, she thought.

"It doesn't matter," Pinch coughed. (He always coughed when he had been sitting on the edge of the mattress for too long). He snuffled and said, "You're right. We'll let it pass," and Peggy realised that he was expecting an answer but she hadn't heard the question.

'The problem is,' she went on thinking. How many times had she begun her soul searching in this way? The problem: she did not know how she was supposed to feel. Just once in her marriage, she had felt excitement but that had been more in expectation of being thrilled rather than the sensation itself. How was she supposed to feel inside herself?

Curiosity, Pinch. That's all it was. I only walked into Macaulay's bedroom because I was curious. But she said nothing out loud.

She heard him belch and move his seat; his digestion was uncomfortable. Peggy pictured it all with her back turned. "Your imposition," he was saying with his fingers at his mouth.

"I've eighty lines to do, my dear," she replied, hoping that her voice didn't tell she was on the edge of tears.

"You must forget it. It's wrong. All wrong." Now he pressed his hands on his knees so that his stomach stretched. Again, he tried hard to bring up some wind. "I don't care who else does that sort of thing. We shouldn't. Not in our house. It's wrong."

She waited for a few moments, then said, "It's our way of putting things right between us. I'd like to finish"

They both waited for the downstairs clock to finish striking half past three. (Sometimes, waiting for the clock to chime made Peggy want to scream in the middle of the night.)

"As you wish," he said, passing her the blame, should anyone think that classroom punishments were peculiar behaviour in a policeman's marriage.

"I've only eighty more lines to complete." How many times did she have to say it?

"We'll not speak of it again."

She felt him lean forward – surely, he was almost touching his toes – but still he couldn't release the trapped wind from his gut.

He said, "I've been thinking about what you found."

"Of course." After all, there was no point in talking about anything else.

"Can you hear me?"

"Of course, dear." Then, realising that she was being told to turn around, she lifted herself on her shoulders, puffed up the feather pillow and sat up. "You're thinking of the covenant and the catapult," she said. (She had not mentioned the Professor's stock of purloined underwear.)

"The Vicar and I questioned him for half an hour. He made no argument about the old deed. He had stolen from the chest when Meggastones was careless. He was quite happy to return it, as long as there was no talk of the matter. Nigel says ..."

"Nigel, dear?"

"The Reverend. Nigel believes that the old fool took it because he loves old things, and I agree. I see no wickedness in it. Ah, but the catapult. Now, there's a different matter. He wriggled like a red-handed thief."

"He stole it from the Dawes' surgery?"

Pinch shook his head. "He said he'd never seen it before. He said he never goes in his back garden and he's no idea how it got there, and I believe him."

"What about the love letters?"

"I can't make sense of it!" Pinch slapped his knee and a trumpet issued from his rear end.

"I've got the letters all wrong," she said quietly. "The Professor didn't write them, but neither did Tilly. She speaks about 'your child' but, I see now, a woman wouldn't say things in that way."

But Pinch was too uncomfortable to listen. "We need to put everyone in their right place at the times of the murders and carefully lay forth the facts. But, always, it ends up the same." He stood up, holding on to the ties of his pyjamas, and looked at his place in the bed. He tried to see his best way of getting into it. "Cover yourself up, Peggy," he directed.

Peggy straightened the blankets, making sure that they weren't showing the line of her bust. She held on tight as Pinch clambered onto the bedstead. He got as far as kneeling on all fours, and seemed content to stay like that for the time being. Bursts of breath kept filling his cheeks. "Always the same." He wanted to talk in short phrases that wouldn't test his tummy's temper. "The people -who were in the right place- to kill both women – had no reason to do so. But people with motives -can give true accounts – of their movements elsewhere." That word, 'movements', seem to trouble him. He sucked in and closed his mouth.

"Then something else does not fit," she sighed, reaching for her detective novel on the lamp table.

Pinch let his arms go, so that his face dropped to the pillow. But his thighs kept his bottom in the air. It was a pantomime posture, as if the front half had forgotten that his back half was supposed to follow. His head was level with her ribs and when he opened one eye, he saw the shape of her breasts beneath her nightdress.

He said, "What do you think?"

"There is one detail," she began, turning from the title page to chapter one. "One, very small, detail. An accidental detail, almost." She ran a finger down the hinge so that the pages lay flat. "No matter how I try, I cannot make sense of it. In the middle of the night, Edie Snag said …"

"She wasn't talking to anyone," Pinch cautioned. Peggy thought that his face was disturbingly red. "She was muttering to herself."

" … that Miss Carstairs knew all about it and she would tell her, the next morning, at half past ten in Bulpit Cottage. But she knew that wasn't true. She knew that Miss Carstairs always goes shopping in town on Tuesday morning."

The stomach cramp was making him cringe. He wanted to arch his back, but didn't know the best thing to do with his legs. He managed to say, "Curious?" Then, because his wife might not have understood him the first time: "You mean curious about how big he was."

Peggy blushed. Oh God, surely she hadn't whispered her thoughts.

"Pinch, I didn't …"

"You did. Under your breath, yes. But you still said it. 'Only because I was curious.' So, you wanted to know if his endowments were greater than mine. Peggy, for God's sake tell me," he winced, one side of his face pressed into his pillow, the other winking involuntarily at Peggy's right breast. "You wanted to tell me yesterday but I wouldn't let you." He was in real pain now. "You're right, five hundred lines puts it right."

"Pinch, yes. I – I caught myself wondering, that's all. But only for a moment and I wasn't thinking straight."

He groaned from the depths and both hands went to his groin. "Do you know who killed Cedar …?"

She laid a hand on his sweat soaked head. "There's something I need to do first, Pinch. Something in the morning, as soon as I've served your breakfast."

He was holding the pit of his belly. "Tell me what I need to know, Peggy," he pleaded.

At once, Peggy realised that he didn't want to hear that Cedar screamed before Peggy had properly looked at Macaulay. The truth would not be enough, but a clever answer now would more than mend any hurt she had caused. How stupid of her not to have realised what really mattered to Mr Pinch.

She remembered what Dorothy had said. 'Comes a time when a girl has to do much better than the truth.' She heard Carstairs' advice. 'You've no talent for composition, Peggity Miller. Speak as it comes.'

Don't think about it, Peggy: "Pinch, he was teeny. You'd have laughed. He was half your size, and hadn't the colour or shape you've got. Really, I can't think his dead mouse had any strength."

She saw that her husband wanted to smile, but the stomach ache wouldn't let him. "Oh God!" he shrieked. "What did that man put in his punch!"

CHAPTER FIFTEEN

King Richard's Castle

The flint and mortar stumps of King Richard's Castle sat on the hillside like old crusty pimples on a labourer's back. But this was no place to build a castle. The ruins were the remnants of a Tudor lodge and not even the most fanciful historian could conjure up a convincing association with either the good King Richard or the bad. The site had been robbed over the centuries; its timbers survived in the walls of Thurrocks' farmhouse and the best stones had been taken for the parish bridge across the Avon stream. However, enough remained to sustain the romance of the place. Ghosts of old England could not have found a better place to muster. Latter day witches had frolicked here on Halloween and the Kindred of Kibbo Kush tramped its boundaries on midsummer night. Mollie Sweatman, Peggy Pinch, Ruby Becker and the Alice sisters remembered picnics here on the last days of term, and who had no memories of the castle during the glorious summer of 1910? For these people, King Richard's Castle was a part of a gone-by but fondly remembered world. For those who had lost sons and brothers, its peacefulness brought thoughts of what might have been. But, of course, each fresh generation came here with new games and sagas.

It was half past ten in the morning and Peggy had been waiting for three quarters of an hour. It was seven days since the killing of Cedar Wells and, although she was sure that the murderer would be taken before lunchtime, her mind was still burdened with business that needed to be settled. Burdened but unmuddled. From now on, the steps towards the arrest would be like a row of matchboxes that could be lightly tipped off a mantelpiece.

On this morning of clear skies and untroubled countryside, even the smallest stir could be noticed and enjoyed, and sounds carried from one side of the picture to the other. Thurrocks farm was two miles away, on the valley's floor, but Peggy could hear clearly the noises of work being done. The squeals of pigs disturbed. The patient efforts of young Rodgers as he tried to turn an old tractor engine. Jones' cart, being drawn in a wide arc from the farmlands towards the village, had disappeared into trees, not seventy yards from Peggy's seat; she could hear the wheels struggling through muddy ruts. An aeroplane was crossing the sky, high up; the engine spluttered, popped and crackled but its cacophonous throat didn't spoil its progress. Peggy looked up and thought how wonderful it must be to fly, free of the earth and regardless of hedges and roads, rivers and hillsides. She remembered her grandmother saying that the first train rides had been just as exciting.

As Mollie's figure emerged from the trees, Peggy saw the schoolgirl who had got her into trouble more than once, the young woman who had put it about that her marriage to Pinch had been a pressing affair, and the scheming gossip who never missed a chance to do her down.

"I'm not going to pay you," Peggy called. "You've already told Pinch that I was in Miss Carstairs' house longer than I should have been."

Mollie just smiled and carried on walking forward. "You think I'm going to let you off."

"Mollie, you were drunk and you shouted it to the village."

"Well, I was right, wasn't I? You did go into Tug's bedroom so that you could see what Pinch couldn't give you."

"I'm not going to pay you," Peggy repeated.

This time Mollie chuckled. "You brought me all the way out here to tell me that?"

"I want to know what you were doing in the Professor's Lodge last night."

"I was spying on you, you stuck-up fool. Can't you see that?"

Peggy chewed her lip. She was sure that she had worked things out right, but Mollie Sweatman always got the better of her. "I don't see it that way at all," she said bluffly. "When you've got something to gossip about, you never give your victim a way out. You like to see them on the edge of tears, squirming and wanting to plead with you. But this time you let me buy your silence. Something's different. Something that you were searching for in The Lodge last night."

"And you expect me to tell you?"

"The Professor is blackmailing you, isn't he? That's why you wanted my money."

"I'd never allow myself to be blackmailed, Peggy Pinch. Not everyone's as weak as you are." But she saw Peggy's scepticism. "OK, I will tell you. Last year, I asked him to draw some pictures of me."

"Pictures?"

"It was my idea," she insisted. "I wanted to show him what a real woman looked like. He's always following you around, stealing a look at you whenever he can. God, it made me sick to see how he was wasting time on you. Don't you see? You're just a dream to him. He'd never want to do anything real with you. So, I laid a little temptation in his way. It was a mistake. He's never asked me to pay for the sketches but I thought I'd get enough money to buy them off him."

"How much?"

"It doesn't matter how much. Don't you see, I didn't care how much; I just wanted it to be your money. I wanted you to pay without knowing what you've done. God, think of the poetry in that!"

"Why not ask me? We don't like each other, Mollie, but I'd always help."

"Oh Lord, that makes me sick! What a dreadful suggestion. You and your precious Miss Carstairs, you think you've been called to sort things out for the rest of us. I can picture you, a pair of holy crows, sharing tea and scones and working out what good work you can do next. I didn't want you to know. I wanted it to be a secret. I wanted to see it work out so that you had to pay for the pictures but couldn't draw any comfort from thinking that you'd done me a good turn. But murder changes things, doesn't it? It can twist people into positions where they might have to own up to little mistakes. That's why I decided that it was simpler to find the drawings and take them for myself."

Peggy wanted to challenge her. These drawings weren't your idea, Mollie Sweatman. Their every pen stroke says that you didn't want to be there. She said, "I'll buy the pictures, Mollie, but not to help you. I'll get the money together, somehow, and I'll pay because the Professor needs protecting from himself. One day, his peculiar ways are going to land him in more trouble than he deserves. He's just a lonely old man."

"Oh, and you know all about old men. Marrying a fool who's older than your father."

"Goodbye, Mollie. We've said all we need to say."

Mollie shook her head. "No. I want to know what you are really scared of, Peggy Pinch. Your husband knows that you walked into Macaulay's bedroom, but still you come out here, asking questions. You want to be sure, don't you? So, what do you really not want me to tell him?"

Peggy kept quiet. She heard Jones' horse tread closer; he was twenty yards off now, close enough to hear.

"It's our night at the Wishing Pool, isn't it?" Mollie prodded.

"That was just an odd little thing that happened."

Peggy turned her back and began to walk from the clearing.

"Well, you certainly know about peculiar little things," Mollie called after her, and when Peggy didn't respond, she added, "Peggy Pinch, how do I know that your husband's got a titchy cock?"

The coarseness riled. Yes, the suggestion that this woman might have seen inside Pinch's trousers worried her, but it was her rude words that made her angry. She turned to face her adversary. Peggy's cheeks burned. Mollie's eyes were fixed, fizzing with laughter, enjoying Peggy's every doubt and discomfort. The women began to circle each other, spacing out an arena in the long grass, avoiding the snares of dead branches and stumps of old trees.

"How would I know?" Mollie repeated, and the women took one step closer, narrowing the circle.

Out of the corner of her eye, Peggy saw the horse and cart on the edge of the clearing, but it made no difference.

"Cock," Mollie teased.

"You always were a filthy girl, Mollie Sweatman. If there was a dirty word in the playground, you had to use it first."

"Cock-a-doodle," Mollie crowed as they circled each other. "How do I know, Peggy? Go on, ask yourself. What makes Mollie say, Pinch has got a weenie cock?"

Peggy's last thought was, if you're going to do it, do it for keeps.

She drew back her arm and smacked Mollie's cheek. The woman went down on one knee, both hands clutching one side of her chin. Her eyes had tears. Her face was contorted.

Peggy spluttered, "You say that word," not knowing what she intended to mean.

Mollie got to her feet, pretended to cower away for a moment, then spun round and bolted an elbow into Peggy's stomach.

Peg bent double, reaching for breath. Then the two women yelped and they were at each other's throats, kicking and punching blindly as they rolled on the grass. They pulled at hair, dug with their nails and trod on what they could reach. They meant to hurt and meant to rub the other's nose into the ground, but there was something satisfying in the moment as if, at last, they were having that fight which they should have had years ago in the playground. Strangely, Peggy wished that Pinch was looking on. This wasn't bad behaviour that she wanted to hide from him or say sorry for. She wanted him, wanted everyone, to see that she was sorting things out.

At first, there was little wickedness in the fight. Whenever Peggy caught a look at Mollie's eyes – just moments in a spin – they were egging her on. But when Mollie spat, she challenged Peggy to break the playground rules with her. Peggy sucked in deep as she made up her mind, then spat back. The dribble, twice as much as Mollie had produced, stuck to the edge of Mollie's lips. When she saw that Mollie was puckering up for a second go, Peggy spat again. Now, the punches were to the face, the digging was in the eyes. Pinches had turned to grips and, when Peggy threw her opponent over her back and through the air, she didn't care about breaking bones.

Mollie was spouting venom. She got to her feet and flung herself at Peggy, who stepped aside and grabbed the woman's dress in full flight. It ripped and when Mollie landed, rolling over, she exposed her leg to its top.

She basked on the ground. "Like it, Peggy? You took naughty looks that night in the Wishing Pool. You said such wonderful things about my body." Again they sprung at each other but, this time, a moment's exhaustion defeated Peggy. Mollie sat astride her chest and pinned her down. "Now." Her eyes glistened. "What else?" She kept Peggy's gaze locked to hers, as she unbuttoned her blouse and, pushing her brassiere aside, exposed a breast. "Come on, Peggy. Take a look. You did then, you know. What do you want to see? Both of them?"

Peggy looked. She had caught Pinch calling them dollopy. When Peggy was alone in the church and the men were working outside, she had overheard Terras and Macaulay laughing over a notion that they had separate names. Flopsy and Mopsy. "Remember that night," whispered Mollie. "Water was falling off them. Christened, you called it. You said they'd been christened with icy drops of witch's water. Is this what you're scared of, scared that Pinch might find out about you?"

With a great thrust of her hips and a twist of her shoulders, Peggy threw her off. They rolled, Peggy not knowing where she was or where she was going, but they ended up with Mollie face down and Peggy lying across the backs of her legs. The woman's dress was torn beyond repair now; it covered nothing up. Peggy gripped the screwed up slip, pushed it up to expose Mollie's old and fraying pants. Before she knew it, Peggy had pulled them down.

Both women were worn out. Mollie couldn't twist or turn; Peggy could hardly lift her head. "Go on, Peg," Mollie was saying. "Go on, girl. Bite it."

Peggy hadn't the strength to do anything else. She squeezed the flesh of Mollie's buttock in one hand, and sunk her teeth in.

Mollie squealed but kicked only listlessly; Peggy held on.

"Harder, Peg."

And Peggy's teeth went into the skin until she could taste it.

"Ah, God! God, please!" Mollie thrashed awkwardly with the last drop of her energy, arching her back, bracing her elbows, tensing her feet, until she lost herself in head-spinning ecstasy. Peggy thought she heard the woman cry 'sorry' and 'never say yield' or, maybe, words of love that made no sense. Peggy went on biting harder and harder. She paused and took a better mouthful. Mollie screeched; she rocked her head, banging it on the ground.

Then, sudden stillness.

A crow commented from a nearby tree. The horse tore a lump of grass from the ground. Mollie's ankle tried to move but fell on its side. Miles away, a motor engine was struggling up a hill.

Peggy withdrew, wiped her mouth and rubbed the aching joints of her neck. She could hear Mollie breathing but she wasn't moving. Now, the indecent state of her clothes shocked Peggy. Limply, she offered a hand to pull a fragment of dress over her thighs, but she thought she'd better not touch.

"Knocked herself out, she has," said Jones. He had drawn the horse and cart to within three yards of the fight. He sat on the driver's bench and puffed on his pipe. "I wouldn't worry about her. She'll have a bump on her head, that's all. Methinks we'd do well to get her in the cart and deliver her back to the village."

"I'd say it were blackmail from the start. Her saying that she wants to buy the drawings is nonsense. She only wants them because she's frit of what he's going to do with them. It's nought to do with me, but I'd say it were blackmail. The young fellow in the Lion were suggesting blackmail, last night, though he'd supped too much to make sense of it. What could our Mollie have on our policeman's wife? Well, the Lord's only knowing that. Nothing improper, I'm not suggesting. It has always seemed to me that you and Arthur Pinch are better suited than most would say."

Jones was a lazy driver. That is to say, the horse knew where she was going and was allowed to take her time getting there. At times, she stopped and bent her neck, as if she were examining the ground close-to. Jones waited patiently for the mare to pull on the cart again. He held the reins lightly in two hands and never seemed to lay any weight on them.

"I've heard say that Doctor Dawes had a busy night. Called to the Vicarage at three o'clock and no later than half past he was with your husband. He had to take advice from the Professor, by all accounts, who told him things would work though before breakfast and the gentlemen should be careful where they drink in future. Would you say that were a true bill o' facts, Mrs Pinch?"

"An accurate account, Mr Jones."

He chuckled. "There's not many who likes you, Mrs Pinch, you'll know that without me saying. The other women, especially. Some of them hate you. Oh-ah, I'd say as far as that. They say you keep yourself back from them. That Pinch-woman thinks she's a cock above us, that's what they say. Call you the Prim-arse, they do. Anyhow, it's all come to a head now. That's what I were thinking when you was fighting back there. This is all part of a come-uppance, your Jonesy was saying to hisself. There's no going back now. There's good money in ladies fighting. Now, our Mollie, no. She's not got the temperament. There'd be no glamour in her fighting. But you? Well, we'd have to arrange it careful and Jonesy'd have to give you some teachering on the noble points. You'll allow you're no boxer just yet a while. But now, well, you keep in mind. Good money. And it's just as those fine gentlemen was saying when they was wanting to fit their racing track on our land. Exploiting the village resources, they called it. Well, it's just the same."

Yes, thought Peggy, comparing the farmer's idea with the Doctor's improper proposal. "It's exactly the same."

"They'll be making it legal, one day. You wait and see. They're opening a dog track in Manchester this month."

"Oh, I'm sure," Peggy said. "Try it with dogs first. Then, if it works, do it with women."

CHAPTER SIXTEEN

Bring Up The Horse!

When the farm track changed into Wretched Lane, Peggy dropped down from the cart. She marched purposefully but she was several paces behind when the horse steered away from the church gate and started down the village street.

Children ran from verges, jumping up at the cart to see inside and shouting the news of what they saw. But not the Willowby pair.

"Oh dear God, please no."

An old square ambulance was stationary at the cottage gate, its back doors open where a stoop-backed old soldier was sorting army blankets. The Vicar, having completed his few words with the attendant, walked slowly away from the cottage, his hands in his pockets. As the horse and cart plodded by, Mrs Willowby came to her front hedge; she looked drawn and sleepless.

John Terras, who had come to board up Bulpit Cottage but had yet to start work, saw Mollie lying in the cart and started to clap. One look from the Doctor put a stop to that. Peggy looked nervously about for Pinch – she hadn't worked out how she was going to explain her latest episode – but she was comforted to see him standing back from the church green with no intention of pushing himself forward. He looked as boring and predictable, as untroubled and lethargic as stodgy pudding. Peggy needed a stodgy pudding that day.

She peeled away from the procession and sat on the War Memorial bench with Miss Carstairs.

"The Medical Superintendent has overruled Doctor Johnny,"

the schoolma'am said. "Grace is to be cared for in hospital. God help the poor child." She sighed. "I'm told it will be another hour before she is moved. There's no talking to Mr and Mrs, quite locked up within themselves."

"We must help in some way."

"Don't play the good citizen, Peggy Pinch. You've been fighting. You'll go too far one day,"

"I wish I'd done it in the ford instead of King Richards, so everyone could have seen. I should have done it years ago."

Miss Carstairs might have nodded, but she didn't speak.

They watched the mock cortège draw up outside Mollie's cottage. She was on her feet, cross and sulky but not wanting to talk. She shrugged away gestures of help from Doctor Dawes and when he persisted, her front door slammed in his face. Less than a minute, and the bedroom curtains were drawn together. She shouted something, but no one understood it (neither were they meant to).

"Yes, the Becker children," Miss Carstairs began. "They show every sign of going wrong, I fear. We all agreed last night that we need to occupy them. God knows why we don't have a Girl Guide Troop. I thought everywhere was supposed to have a Girl Guide Troop these days."

"Dorothy Becker's a good girl," Peggy insisted.

"Yes, yes. With a steady hand. "

"I know what you're thinking. If you were still the schoolmistress you'd get them working on a May Pole or a festival. But you can't step in the way of your successor."

"Different. Very different." She inhaled, raising her heavy chest. "I mustn't interfere"

Peggy spoke to the clouds. "I said I'll look after Dorothy. She'll grow up, just fine."

The Jones cart was standing in the ford, the horse enjoying the cool water, the farmer eating his bread cobs, marrow and cheese on the driving seat. He had paid a lad a halfpenny to fetch a quart of beer from the Red Lion's back door. John Terras was sitting on the porch of Bulpit cottage, with his packed lunch spread across his lap. Peggy heard someone pass through the kissing gate, a hundred yards behind her, and she guessed that Alice Tarporley's mother was taking her knitting bag into the church. The place often provided her with a few quiet moments after her morning chores. Mrs Willowby, without her children, crossed The Street to the Post Office but went round the back rather than through the shop's front door. The Doctor was sorting maps on the bonnet of his Silent Six at the roadside and, Peggy knew, Pinch would already be looking forward to his nap on the parlour couch.

"It's time we did something about our Professor," the schoolma'am announced. "We can't ignore the items you found in his house. His little trinkets." She explained, "I suppose you wanted to keep them secret, but Dorothy Becker has already told me."

"I didn't want to tell Pinch. I thought that the Professor deserves some privacy, but Pinch got the better of me last night."

"I'm sure that he had nothing to do with poor Cedar's death but we can't allow things to fester."

Peggy agreed. Because Miss Carstairs was playing at schoolteacher, she wanted to stay obediently quiet, but there was too much that needed saying. "We've always said that the village is divided between the rich people who live on the edges and the rest of us in the middle. Well, I think it's worse. I think the men live on one side of The Street and we live on the other. It's all about men fighting women."

"Nonsense, child. It's nothing about that. It's about keeping people on the outside. Do you remember when I scolded you for saying that old Miss Smithers was a witch?"

"You gave me the stick in front of the other children. Of course, I remember. They made up that horrid rhyme and they've whispered it ever since. It's cruel."

"I said that folk told stories about the poor woman because the village kept her in the cold. We wanted nothing to do with her."

"We all knew that there was quite a to-do about it. Grown-ups came to your cottage that night and all the lights were on. Mollie Sweatman said her father was shouting that you weren't fit to teach children."

"Foolish man. Yes, there was quite an argument and, I'm afraid, it only made matters worse for poor Miss Smithers. She was driven from the village. Well, we cannot make the same mistake with the Professor. He must be brought inside. I've already taken steps. Miss Mullens has agreed that the Professor will take charge of the pictures. He will review the Red Lion's wall each month and offer advice. Where possible, he will be in charge of procurement."

"Supply," Peggy muttered to herself.

"Quite right, Peggy. Procurement and supply will give him something to bother about. Furthermore, Verger Meggastones, Mrs Willowby and I will sit with the Professor one afternoon each week. Taking turns. I would like you to play a hand, Peggy. The Professor trusts you."

"Yes, Miss Carstairs."

"There remains the question of his Lodge. We need to keep an eye on it, Peggy, so I've a mind to ask Alice Tarporley to clean for the Professor, three mornings a week. We will need to pay her, of course. I hear that the sweethearts are saving up."

"The library fund, Miss Carstairs."

"Whatever's up with you, Peggy. You're talking like one of my pupils. We're not in school now." Then she tutted to herself. "Yes, perhaps I am announcing after prayers again. I must stop it."

"We've always liked you to."

The schoolma'am didn't mention that she had received a nonsense letter from the Professor, accusing her of helping to hide Mr Pinch's dubious history. She wouldn't do anything with it until the murders were settled. The note was tucked away, ready to confront their peculiar Professor when he was feeling better. "I've already spoken to the Vicar. He feels it would be quite in order to put aside part of the library fund, and I'll see that the Professor donates some volumes from his own library in consideration. Yes, all in all, a very tidy arrangement."

Peggy tried to remember her geometry lessons. "Symmetrical," she said.

"I don't think so, Peggy. I don't think 'symmetrical' at all." The old lady gathered her handbag and coat and, getting to her feet, said, "You may want to stay behind and chalk 'reciprocal' twenty times on the blackboard."

171

But Peggy's missed the teasing; her mind was elsewhere. "Miss Carstairs, it's time that people knew the truth. If I let matters rest, worse will come of it."

"You know who killed Cedar Wells?"

"I'm sure of it. Sadness and secrets have led to these murders and the longer the mystery remains unsolved, the more people will be damaged."

"Do be careful, Peggy."

Peggy got to her feet, waited for Miss Carstairs to indicate that she would follow, then walked slowly down the middle of The Street. John Terras had finished his tuck and was about to get back to work but, sensing that something important was going on, stepped out into the road as the two women arrived at the front gate of School Cottage. The spot where, one week ago, Cedar Wells had fallen.

Driver David, soiled and greasy from working on the motorbus, was the next to join them, and Verger Meggastones. Mrs Willowby, determined that her children should hear nothing, went through her rooms, shutting all the windows. Presently, she opened one at the top of her stairs and peered out. Pepys did the same, across the road at the Red Lion. So, slowly and without being called, the villagers mustered. The Professor, appearing from nowhere as usual. The Vicar, coming out of Bulpit Cottage, where no one knew he had been. The Postmistress, and Miss Mullens and Mr Lovely of the Red Lion, left their businesses open and unattended. And the two lovers, Alice Tarporley and Michael, emerged from the hazel alley, sheepishly, for they had clearly been courting.

Perhaps the appearance of the Beckers was the most curious. Dorothy had been collecting stones in the hedgebottom at the Police House when she saw the village assembling. She ran up The Street shouting for her parents. Something that Dorothy Becker rarely did. The grown-ups brought Freddie and the four of them stood on the edge of the little crowd.

By the time Pinch and Doctor Dawes came walking up from the ford, nearly twenty people had gathered around Peggy Pinch and the old schoolmistress. And Mollie Sweatman, bruise or no bruise, wasn't slow to be on the scene. "My God, she's going to tell!" she giggled to herself, hurrying so much that she left her front door and front gate open. "She's really going to say what she was up to when Cedar was done in." She caught Mr Lovely by the sleeve. "She is, she's going to tell." She pushed herself excitedly to the front.

Peggy began, when her husband was close to her, "We all agree that Cedar was hit by a stone, thrown from a first floor window. But Pinch is right. The murderer could not have been in Old School Cottage. Look." She raised an arm towards the bedroom where she had spied on Tug Macaulay. "Macaulay could only have struck the back of Cedar's head if she had already passed the cottage. She would have needed to be thirty or forty yards from where she fell."

The villagers lifted their heads and looked around. "Aye, that's right enough," said Verger Meggastones. "It's the top of the Red Lion. Standing here, it's clear. The stone could only have been thrown from the front bedrooms of The Red Lion."

"It wasn't me!" young Pepys shouted at the top of his voice. He slammed the window shut and ran down the stairs, all the time shouting so everyone could hear, "I promise, I wasn't in the village that morning!"

"I know, Pepys," said Peggy. She paused and looked at each face in the crowd. "The truth is that any of us could have climbed the Red Lion staircase." She took one step towards the Doctor. "Harold Dawes, here. Our good Doctor. He didn't want Cedar to talk about their improper arrangement. He had been paying for Cedar's company for months."

"A slander!"

"But of course, that would be no motive for murder, would it, Doctor? You felt safe enough to make the same awful proposal to me, sure that I would tell no one or, if I did, I would carry the blame. No, that was no reason to kill Cedar. No reason at all."

"This is quite scurrilous. Everybody, you must take this for nothing more than slander!"

But the blank faces soon told the Doctor that the neighbours were in a mood to listen.

"Pinch is right," repeated the policeman's wife. "If we want to make sense of this, we must look for something that doesn't make sense. Our Reverend was told that Edie Snag said ..."

The Vicar interrupted her. "Please, Mrs Pinch. Have a care for the innocent."

"Edie Snag said, 'Miss Carstairs knows the truth. She'll tell everyone tomorrow.' But that is nonsense. Edie knew that Miss Carstairs couldn't show the village anything that morning because she and Miss Carstairs had already agreed to meet in town, in the library."

"Ah!"

"Yes, Doctor. That was my mistake. I thought 'the library' meant Bulpit Cottage."

"No, no," said Miss Carstairs, now intrigued by the evolving solution. "The library in town. I made that clear to Edie. I wanted to explain to her about raising the subscriptions."

Peggy turned to the Vicar. " 'Miss Carstairs knows the truth. She'll tell everyone tomorrow.' Who told you that?"

"No, no. I can't share that!"

Ruby Becker reached out a limp hand. "Oh, Peggy, please don't involve my poor girl."

"We don't need to." Peggy spoke slowly. She wanted everyone to follow what she was saying. She noticed that old Gregory, the neighbourhood tramp had settled himself on the opposite verge, his coats, scarves and sacks making a spreading camp. "Let's just change a few words. Well, not the words, but let's change what we think they mean. Edie didn't mean that Miss Carstairs would show anything; she knew that Miss Carstairs wouldn't be here. The murderer has made sure that Edie is not here to explain but, surely, she meant Miss Carstairs knows everything and Cedar will show everything."

"Cedar was going to show that she's a woman," the Doctor exclaimed. "That's the only way it makes sense."

"Where does that get us?" Pinch began. But then he took off his helmet, scratched his scalp and smiled; Peggy saw that her husband had worked it out. "How clever of you, my dear," he said.

"You must explain it, Pinch, not me."

Pinch proceeded carefully, checking his reasoning as he went along. "Someone else heard Edie's words and thought they knew exactly what she meant, and it was nothing about Cedar's dressing up as a man. That person made up their mind to murder Cedar before she could reveal all that she knew. Ruby Becker, I saw your young 'un hiding in the bushes when Edie was rambling."

"The library," the Vicar insisted. "Edie was upset about the library and she was muttering to herself. About the library!"

Pinch nodded. He was almost chuckling now. "That's what the young child thought, but she was wrong. Thank God, the truth was way beyond her understanding. I couldn't hear Edie clearly because I had crossed Verger Meggastones' garden toward the footpath. I was, I'm sorry to say, still envious of the pigeon manure."

"Hardly makes you a murderer, Pinch!" declared the Doctor.

Now it was the Vicar's turn to feel that too many accusing eyes were turned on him. "Do you think I was making it up? I wasn't there."

"No one thinks that, old man," said Dawes. "But it would be foolish to rely on something overheard by a child. That's all we're saying."

No one noticed the resentment on little Dorothy Becker's face. She had turned to the Vicar in secret on that awful night and he had promised to keep it secret. Now, the Doctor was calling her a fibber.

"I was confused as anyone would have been. I was only repeating …" The Vicar looked from face to face. "Good Lord," he said quietly, "why would I kill anyone?" He frowned as he tried to work it out. "I didn't know anything about the village secrets. I even went to Dawes and told him how puzzled I was. Dawes, tell them. Tell them I was confused by it all."

"Just so," said Pinch, without turning to the Doctor, and he looked to Peggy for support.

"Just so," she agreed. "But you told our Doctor what Dorothy had reported, and our Doctor knew exactly what Cedar was about to reveal, and he knew that someone needed to silence poor Edie if we weren't to solve the mystery. The letters …"

"No!" The Professor jumped forward. "Nothing to do with me! Yes, I did take the letters. No, I shouldn't have done but, yes, I did."

"When you were scavenging in Bulpit Cottage," said Peggy, "in those few days in 1912 after Tilly Peters had left but before Edie moved in."

"What letters?" three people asked at once.

Pinch had run out of steam. Again, Peggy took up the explanation. "They are little more than notes, sent to a lover, asking that they should meet at the back of Bulpit Cottage. I noticed that they weren't written in the Professor's copperplate but that seemed to make sense. I thought that they were Tilly's letters to the Professor."

The Professor was shaking his head. "But I found the letters amongst her possessions. They weren't letters she sent, they were letters she received."

"Of course," Peggy agreed. "They were notes sent by the man to the woman. If we examine the handwriting then we will learn the identity of the lover."

"Will that tell us who killed Cedar Wells?" Miss Carstairs asked.

Jones brought his horse to attention and, with a lazy effort, the mare pulled the cart from the ford and began a slow clip-clop up The Street. Jones kept the lead in one hand and his beer in the other.

"Let's do it," exclaimed the Vicar. "The letters, the handwriting, here and now!"

The Doctor pushed himself to the front. "It wouldn't help us, I'm afraid. Medical knowledge has asserted that anyone can forge a letter, and what could we make of handwriting that's fifteen years old? Very little, I'm afraid. I'm sorry, Peggy, but your evidence is really no evidence at all."

The Vicar clapped his hands to his sides. "If we don't do something, we'll accuse the wrong person!"

"I don't think so," Peggy assured him.

The horse had built up a brisk pace now; Jones steadied her. They were less than fifty yards off.

Peggy held her hands open. "Vicar, when you reported to Doctor Dawes that Miss Carstairs knew everything and she would tell us all in the morning, it was like a nightmare becoming real. Doctor, you understood, before any of us, that 'she will tell everything' referred to Cedar. But nothing about her dressing up. What other secret could Cedar reveal?"

Peggy waited for the villagers to absorb her explanation.

"She had been friends with Pepys' mother for many years. Had she been told the identity of the father?"

"Of course," Miss Carstairs said quietly. "He feared that Cedar – the one person in a position to know too much – had learned about his affair with Tilly. He feared that the secret that Cedar would expose the next day was the same secret that Tilly had so loyally kept for fifteen years. The identity of your father, young Pepys."

Before the youth had time to react, Dawes thrashed out, determined to be free of the crowd. But Meggastones and Pinch had stationed themselves at his back and soon had him in their grip.

"You had Dorothy's catapult and you aimed from the inn's bedroom." Peggy was speaking quickly now, almost shouting at the man under arrest. "Then you ran down the wobbly path and came sauntering up from the bottom of the village, a direction that nobody thought the murderer would come from. Later, you entered The Lodge and hid the catapult in the Professor's garden. You killed poor Edie before morning, and you thought that no one would suspect if you were the one to find her body."

"Nonsense!" cried the Doctor.

The Vicar had fixed his eyes on the suspect. "The handwriting will show," he said, no more shrill than thinking aloud.

"It would have been different if I had found those letters!" roared Dawes, his face white, his eyes wide. "The stupid girl! Why did she keep the damned letters!"

Then the four Beckers ran for him and, in the scuffle to keep them off, Dawes broke free. "Let's have it out, Pinch!" he yelled as he started to run.

"No pursuit!" commanded Pinch as he lay on the ground. He shouted it again as the Vicar and Verger helped him to his feet. But Dorothy Becker had already jumped on the back of the cart, hallowing a war-cry that stirred Farmer Jones into action. He cracked the reins and the seasoned mare took up the chase.

Peggy couldn't bear seeing the child at risk again, just one week after she had been unconscious in the tree tops. The policeman's wife flung herself at the tailgate of the wagon and hauled herself aboard.

The village waved and cheered, hallowing "Three cheers for Peggy," like they'd read in school stories.

Dorothy shouted through the noise, "He used what I said, Aunt Peggy! I said it and he used it to kill Miss Cedar and poor Edie."

Peggy held the girl close with one hand and clutched the side of the cart with the other. "He hurt me too, Dorothy." They were standing up straight, like a brace of Boadiceas. "We'll catch him together."

Everyone thought that the Doctor would make for his car, but he didn't. He kept running up hill until his pace weakened and his shoulders slumped. At the church green, he turned and waved his arms defiantly. He shouted in despair, but then a second yell was in angry defiance. Jones was driving too fast and too close to avoid him and the Doctor didn't try to jump out of the way. He screamed from the bed of his lungs and, at the very last moment, tripped backwards and sprawled beneath the horse's hooves. He rolled and the cart's last wheel went over his back.

The body was left kicking and jerking like a broken rabbit in the road. Peggy and Dorothy were in tears and Jones was off the wagon, striding towards the casualty. The first of the crowd was already with them. But nobody spoke. At that moment, the parish clock struck one, people looked towards the tower and an eerie quiet lay over the scene.

It was a hideous death. It stunned the villagers. Ruby Becker gathered her family around her, Terras helped the farmer put his cart in order and Postmistress Mary went to Mollie's aid. She was being sick at the roadside, her bile mixed with the dregs of her tears and specks of blood from a bitten lip. These things went on without a word. The Vicar, Miss Carstairs, Pinch and Peggy stayed a few paces apart and looked at what had happened. There was an uncomfortable feeling that the village hadn't done well. It was as if the Doctor's soul had risen up, spilling his wickedness on the ground where he had lived. Something like, the evil that men do lives on after them. No one was sure that they weren't dirty with it. Murder wouldn't come to a clean and healthy place, but it had visited their community; they had found out the culprit and run him down. The villagers shared an unspoken notion that the picture had a medieval taste. Could any of them say that they wouldn't have stoned the bad Doctor Dawes, given the chance?

The Willowby ambulance started up quietly and drove away from the village, through the ford at the bottom of the hill, avoiding the mess at the top. Miss Carstairs collected Peggy's arm. As they walked down The Street, they remarked that the Professor had made himself scarce and Seth Lovely had taken his grandson into the Red Lion.

PEGGY PINCH, POLICEMAN'S WIFE
Malcolm Noble
Matador Paperback
ISBN: 9781848767867

Peggy Pinch, unhappily married to the village policeman, must solve a murder to save her husband's job.

It's 1926. In the shadow of the General Strike, a local farmer is found dead on the neighbourhood branch line. Scotland Yard's investigation threatens to uncover parish scandals and gossip that will discredit PC Pinch. Peggy has no doubt; she must catch the killer within a few days, or the couple will lose their home and be driven from the village where she has lived all her life.

"This fantastic village whodunnit. Malcolm Noble's story is intricately plotted, suspenseful, darkly funny, and beautifully written, leading inexorably towards the clever denouement. I loved it. I will read more."

(Historical Novel Society)